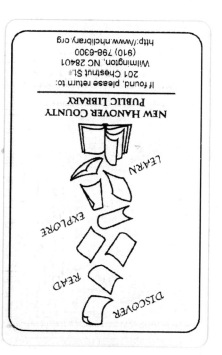

NAKED MOON

ALSO BY DOMENIC STANSBERRY

NAKED
MOON

Domenic Stansberry

 MINOTAUR BOOKS ⚹ NEW YORK

This is a work of fiction. All of the characters, organizations, and events portrayed in this novel are either products of the author's imagination or are used fictitiously.

www.minotaurbooks.com

Library of Congress Cataloging-in-Publication Data

Stansberry, Domenic.
    Naked moon / Domenic Stansberry.—1st ed.
        p. cm.
    ISBN 978-0-312-36454-0
    1. Private investigators—Fiction.   I. Title.
    PS3569.T3335N35 2010
    813'.54—dc22
                                    2009041527

First Edition: March 2010

10   9   8   7   6   5   4   3   2   1

Sunshine isn't enough.

—Nathanael West

PART ONE

PART ONE

ONE

Dante Mancuso lay on the dead woman's bed, listening to the alley. The previous tenant, an old woman, had collapsed on the stairs of the hotel some days before, but the room had not been cleaned out. Her spotted dishes were in the drainboard, and an unfinished meal in the refrigerator. This part of town, management was not concerned with such details. Ultimately, neither was Dante. He had other reasons for being here. No matter the dead woman's reading glasses rested on the bed stand, next to his revolver, and her clothes still hung in the closet.

He picked up the gun and eased toward the window.

Pigeons scuttered and cooed along the sill, and so he moved cautiously. He didn't want to rile the birds or call attention to his form behind the tattered sheers.

The hotel stood just off Portsmouth Square, in Chinatown, and noise from the square echoed down the narrow alley. It traveled oddly, so that individual sounds—coughing, footsteps, snatches of talk—were unnaturally distinct yet somehow disembodied, their origins hard to trace. At the same time, he could hear one of Ching Lee's rally trucks. The mayoral candidate had a number of such vehicles working the neighborhood: old Fords, loudspeakers planted on the hood, rollicking in Chinese.

For a moment it sounded as if this truck were right out front, then no . . . maybe Stockton Street. . . .

It was hard to tell how close . . . how far. . . .

But through all that noise, he had heard, he was all but certain, the clanging of an iron gate.

D ante Mancuso had checked in the night before, but he hadn't given his real name. The hotel was nameless, or rather had too many names for any of them to be useful. An engraving in the cornerstone called it the Fortunato Building—named after some Italian immigrant, long since forgotten—but the fading lettering on the side entrance called it the Three Prosperities.

Meanwhile, a sign hung from the side corner, Chinese writing, neon, glass broken, shattered in such a way that the underlying ideogram—whatever it might have been—was no longer decipherable.

There was no front desk, in the traditional sense, just a clerk in the gimcrack shop below, in what used to be the building's lobby. The clerk had given him a stamped receipt with no information other than the date, and even that was not legible.

In his other life—his real life, as it might be called—
Dante lived not so far away, just the other side of Columbus,
in what remained of the Italian neighborhood. He had made
his way over to the hotel by means of an elaborate dodge,
but in the end he had no idea if the ruse had worked. It
might have been wiser to take up residence at someplace
more distant, but he first had an errand to run and needed
to be here, in Chinatown, within striking distance of the
Wu Benevolent Association.

Rumor had it that Teng Wu, the founder of the association, still lived in the upper story. Or Love Wu, as the man
was known.

Other rumors had it Wu died long ago.

Now a large pigeon flew onto the sill, scattering the
smaller birds. Dante stood behind the sheers, peering
down, gun in hand. The sky was still blue and brilliant
overhead—too blue, it seemed, too brilliant. Closer down,
dusk had gathered in the alley and the shadows darkened.
Emerging from these shadows was the figure of an old Cantonese, who by some special arrangement had a key to the
iron gate and lived at the end of the alley.

The alley led back behind the tenement, growing nar-
rower with each turn, eventually ending in a patch of pave-
ment, a dead end, cloistered in on three sides by brick
buildings. The Chinaman kept his bedroll there, and a
small cookstove, and a container of food with a plastic top
to keep out the rats.

Earlier, exploring the alley, Dante had come across the old man at the end of the alley in the lotus position, meditating, humming one of those low Buddhist chants that was like a noise from the center of the earth.

Aside from the alley—which offered no real exit—there were two other ways out of the hotel. One down a narrow set of stairs that opened onto Grant. The other by means of a wide staircase that descended into the gimcrack shop below.

D ante had come here dressed like a workingman who had suffered some bad luck, self-inflicted or otherwise. Pants too big, loose at the hips, fabric worn and shiny at the knees. A gray work shirt buttoned to the collar. He looked like himself but not himself. He also wore sunglasses and a painter's cap. At a glance, he fit in well enough—his expression was drawn, and he had the hunched look of a convict. But his face gave a lie to the whole thing. He was still recognizable up close, if for no other reason than his nose.

The large Italian nose—from his mother's side—dignified or absurd, depending upon how you viewed things.

A nose like Caesar, his grandmother used to say. Like some long-dead Italian pope. Like Pinocchio, trapped inside the belly of a fish.

The joke in the middle of this face.

H e stripped off his clothes and lay back down in the dead woman's bed, listening. He had not slept much the last few days and did not know if he would ever sleep again. He carried a vial of amphetamines in his pocket but yearned for sleep.

He had a longing in him he could not describe. He was thinking of the dead. He was thinking of the old-timers who had walked these streets before. The Irish dead and the Italian dead and the German Jews, all with their demon smiles and fat suspenders, fresh from the two-dollar whorehouse that used to be around the corner from the Hall of Justice, on the other side of the square, before they'd torn down the station and the morgue and moved it all South of Market. A cement-colored hotel stood there now, towering over the men playing mah-jongg.

Dante was thinking of the life he had not meant to live, but lived anyway. Of the people he had helped along into the land of the dead.

Of people he himself had killed and those whom he had caused to be killed. He was thinking of his cousin, the fool, lying on the floor with the big gash around his neck. Of his boss at the agency, Jake Cicero. And of a woman in a white dress. He imagined her in a place far away. A place that was like this place, but not like here. Foreign tongues and the smell of tropical flowers, and dark alleys that opened into a sunlit plaza underneath a church with high spires. Behind his closed eyes the woman emerged from one of those alleys into the plaza, standing in her white dress at the stairs at the foot of the church.

Meanwhile, overhead, that same sky . . . too blue . . . too beautiful. . . .

There was no escape.

If he did not run their errand, if he refused, his old friends would kill him. But he knew, too, on the other hand, if he cooperated, once the errand was done, they had no intention of letting him walk away.

He had a third alternative.

He could flee.

He had lived underground, and he could get another identity. He could hide indefinitely. But even if he were able to hide, the same was not true of the woman in the white dress.

They would find her. And he would die another kind of death.

TWO

Two weeks earlier, Dante had stood with his back to the window—in the family house on Fresno Street. He had not known what was coming then, though perhaps he should have known. He had started out with SFPD after all, and worked as an investigator now. Then there were those long years in between—years he did not talk about—when he'd worked out of New Orleans. Regardless, his attention that night had been in front of him. He peered across the darkness of his father's old bedroom at the woman sitting there at the edge of the mattress, knees crossed.

Her name was Marilyn Visconti. They had known each other since they were young.

"So what have you decided?" she asked.

Since his father's death, Dante had rented the place out off and on, and the latest tenants had left a box spring on the floor. Three years now since the old man's death—tenants had come and gone—but Dante had not yet cleared out his parents' belongings. The attic and the basement were still littered with his parents' stuff.

"Nothing. I'm just going through their things."

Marilyn and Dante had conversations like this, more or less, every time the house went vacant. The radio crackled with a nostalgic tune, from a warbler whose name had been well known in his parents' prime but that now was pretty much forgotten. There was a noise on the street, and a creaking on the inside stairs, but these were familiar sounds. There were always noises out in the street. The house always creaked.

Meanwhile, Marilyn sat on the edge of the bed in a loose-fitting shift, her face in the shadows, away from the hard light falling through the window. She was an old-fashioned-looking girl some ways, with a body that had some handle to it, full lips, dark hair. Her face was scarred, though, and there were suture marks, the result of an accident—a fire, some time back now, almost a year, that had broken out unexpectedly at a legal fund-raiser out in Oakland. She'd gotten good care and learned, too, the art of applying Lycogel, the burn makeup. He could not see her scars from where he stood, across the darkened room, but they were still there, he knew, and there was more scarring along her abdomen, her arms, on the thighs underneath the black tights.

"I guess there's no rush," she said.

"No."

"But this place—it could use some paint, at least."

He and Marilyn had been together off and on. He'd

known her before he'd gone away, and after he came back, and they'd put each other through the usual kinds of difficulties, but there was still, despite everything, the same electricity between them. She was in her mid-thirties, some five years younger than himself.

"I guess it depends on how you want to live. If you mean to rent the place out, or live here yourself . . ."

They did not talk about the fact that Marilyn had been gone for the last ten days. Dante did not ask and she had the delicacy not to tell him, though he knew well enough.

She'd been to Santa Barbara—in the company of David Lake.

David Lake was a widower, a few years older than Dante, who had taken an interest in her after the accident.

Wrong place, wrong time.

My fault, Dante thought, because he'd taken her to Oakland that night. Because the event had been in behalf of some client at Cicero's Investigations, where Dante worked. Dante and Marilyn did not talk about that, however, nor did they talk about David Lake. They talked instead about the empty house, and about his parents. They talked about his cousin Gary, who was having legal troubles out at the warehouse, and about Gary's wife, Viola, who wanted a divorce, and wanted it now, before the Feds moved in and took everything. They talked about his grandfather's old felucca, a small sailboat of the sort once used by the Sicilian fishermen. It sat unused in a slip down at the Marina, and it was one of the things Dante had resolved to let go.

"The buyer, he's taking title Saturday."

"Are you going to take it out one last time?"

"Maybe."

"You should."

"It's an idea."

"It's nice out there, on the water."

"Friday?"

Marilyn had grown close to David Lake, Dante knew. Before the accident, she worked down at Prospero Real Estate, and Lake had gone to her with some property he wanted to sell. Whether there had been anything between them back then, Dante wasn't sure. Either way, Lake had money—and after the incident, arranged for an eye specialist, then trips down to Los Angeles to a plastic surgeon. The surgeon was one of the best. She was lucky her injures were not worse. Lucky, too, that the widower David Lake had taken an interest in seeing her mend.

It was not an unselfish interest, but few things were.

She had most all her vision in one eye, but the other one was glass—or plastic, more accurately, as that was the way they made them now, with some kind of material in the artificial surface designed to mimic the good eye, so both eyes appeared to shift and track. The effect was imperfect at times, disconcerting.

"We could take the boat out to Angel Island," Dante said. "The weather's been good."

Angel Island was an uninhabited island in the middle of the bay. They used to take the boat out when they were younger and things had been simpler between them. Cut the engine. Let it drift.

"What did the doctor say?" he asked. Her eyes skittered over him, the good eye and the bad eye.

"It's coming along."

The surgeries were over. This latest examination could have been done locally, but Lake had taken her down to the specialist's clinic in Ysidro, at an old ranch in the Santa Barbara foothills. A healing resort. Mud baths and physical therapists and the swimming pool where Carole Lombard once swam. Ysidro was where the Hollywood people went these days to recuperate after plastic surgery.

"Let me see," he said.

She had a primness that had not been there before and stiffened, just a little, when he reached toward her. He reached anyway and put a finger on her lips, just touching, then brushed the hair back from her face. Despite her involvement with David Lake, they were still intimate from time to time. They kissed, and he felt a sharp desire and for an instant imagined a distant shore someplace, an ancient alley, the cathedral in a picture she had shown him once upon a time. She had told him—self-deprecating, laughing at herself—how she used to imagine, when she was a girl, that she would get married in Italy, in a picture like that. But that was some time ago when she told him that, and they had both been a lot more innocent then, lying together fully dressed, legs twisted, chests pushed one against the other, and he pulling up her shirt so he could press her stomach to his. They lay on the bed now, similarly entangled, but they were—both of them—thinking about David Lake.

Dante lifted his head, and she pulled away, lying beside

him but not touching. She petted his enormous nose for a little while, but it was more like the petting you would give a lost dog. He walked away to the window and lit a cigarette and stared down into the shadows.

"He asked me to marry him," she said.

She sat on the edge of the bed, knees together. Her blouse was open, unbuttoned at the top, and she wore a camisole beneath. The clothes were new. Purchased in a boutique down in Santa Barbara, maybe. She and David Lake, out shopping. A moment before, he had been running his hands up over her slacks. Expensive. He liked the feel of them, of running his hands up over the fabric, over the zipper at the front, feeling the warmth beneath. He was tempted to get on his knees now and crawl back to where she was and put his head down so he could bury his nose in the fabric between her legs.

David Lake.

She regarded Dante with the dead eye. The oracular eye. Reading his mind, maybe. Glimpsing for an instant all that stuff inside. He wondered what she saw, but in truth, the good eye was downcast, and it was just the other eye, stubborn, confused by the darkness. Not following its mate.

His cell phone sat on the table next to the bed. The ringer was off, but it started to vibrate, shaking, a thrumming noise, small-throated, persistent.

That was when it had all started, he would think later. With the shaking of the phone on the tabletop. That was the moment leading to the moment when he would find himself at the nameless hotel. When he would hear at once the old Buddhist moaning in the alley and the assassin's cord whipping the air behind him and see the flames rising at his feet. The moment in which you saw backward and forward and realized there was no such thing as time, no such thing as space, only the instant of death. All of life was spent in this instant, but he did not see this now, not yet. He saw only Marilyn sitting there on the bed.

"Gary?" she asked.

It was a reasonable guess. His cousin had left him a number of messages these past days, his voice more urgent with each call. There had been some kind of scene, Dante knew, out at Rossi's place, between his cousin and Joe Rossi, the former mayor, whose daughter was running for office. Then there was this new man Gary had been meeting with, Dominick Greene.

"Is it your cousin?"

"I don't think so."

"Work?"

"Maybe."

The number was not one Dante recognized, but this was often true in his line of work. Some of Cicero's clients were not particularly savory, and they used disposable phones that were difficult to trace. Either way, he decided not to pick up, not now. He looked at Marilyn across the room.

I am going to get on the floor, he thought. *I am going to drop to my knees and crawl.*

"I should get going," she said.

"Angel Island?" he asked "Friday—"

"I'll check with the office. I have a new listing to prepare . . . and there's this couple looking for a place."

"A couple?"

"New in town. They want to buy."

"Let me walk you home."

"No. I'll be all right."

"Just to the corner."

"I've lived in this neighborhood my whole life."

"Then you know how it can be."

"I'll be okay."

"Just to the corner."

THREE

When the phone rang again, he was alone. Marilyn was gone and he stood in the basement, looking at the things his parents had left behind. Inside a small wooden box, of the type that required careful handling, he found their wedding rings. Other boxes held old clothes, papers, a plethora of shoes. He had to decide what to keep, what to throw away. Before his mother died, she'd been tormented by voices, by all those things in the attic, their secrets, the past, conspiracies she could not decipher. He remembered his father putting his hands over her ears.

Don't Listen.

Dante put down the box with the rings and answered the phone.

On the other side, the line sounded dead at first, in the background a faint clicking, erratically spaced, like the noise of an old-fashioned Teletype—the electronic humming of an encrypted line. Then the voice—the same voice that had contacted him in the past, during those years he did not talk about. Whether the voice was male or female, he had never been able to tell. Filtered, for security purposes, so the identity could not be decoded. Throatless, reedy, not quite human. A sound like an insect speaking through a megaphone.

"We have an unpaid invoice."

"I don't know what you're talking about."

"That isn't the answer we want."

"No?"

"It's not what we are hoping for."

Dante was tempted to pull off the phone, to hang it up, but in the end, he knew, it would not do any good, and there was—in the ugliness of the voice, the coercive thrumming, the cell phone darkness—a hypnotic quality.

"I am speaking to Mr. Pelican?" the insect asked. It was a nickname, passed on to Dante from his mother's side—on account he had inherited his grandfather's ungainly nose. "Son of Giuseppe Mancuso and Marie Pelicanos, yes?" Dante did not answer. "We have the right man, I am sure. Grandson of fishermen. Nose of noses."

There was, on the one hand, a protocol, a means of identification expected when you talked to the company, but there had always been, on the other hand, a mocking quality about this protocol, the sense the rules applied only in one direction. Dante had broken from the company, something not easily done.

"They have passed on, I know. But you have people you love, don't you. A life that you want to live."

I should have walked Marilyn home, he thought. I should not have let her go on alone.

"What do you want?"

"I think you know."

With SFPD, Dante had worked his way to homicide, but eventually things had gone askew, and he'd found another way of making a living. Corporate security, he'd told people, for an export firm in New Orleans, and though there was an element of truth, the firm was a shill, a front for intelligence operations several steps removed, taking place in a gray area where the players were untraceable and the intentions hard to sort. His last case, three years ago, had brought him back here, to San Francisco, and he'd managed, through a kind of uneasy truce, to break free. He'd committed certain transgressions to do so, and the act of breaking free was a transgression in itself, and he'd feared, sooner or later, that this moment might come that it would be wiser to leave the city, to forget his old life and disappear—but he'd lingered nonetheless.

"You have a cousin, too, don't you? Then there's that partner of yours."

"What about them?"

"You've been double-dipping."

"No."

"Someone has. Playing it two ways. Revealing information to both sides."

"That's not possible."

"Mind your cousin."

"He knows nothing."

"There are others you care about?"

The insect fell silent, so there was only the ticking on the line. The past circling back. It was a lulling, hypnotic silence. I've lingered too long, he thought. Still, what the voice suggested was impossible. He had not divulged anything to anyone. His own mother had gone mad in this house, hearing voices. Whispers in the creaking stairs. Conspirators in the plaster.

He wondered what exactly had happened out at Rossi's, with his cousin Gary, and he wondered, too, about his cousin's new friend, Dominick Greene, the importer here on a working holiday, checking out shipping and storage supposedly, but spending a lot of time in the bars. Dante had run into Greene with his cousin in the square, then seen him around the neighborhood several times since. Coincidence, perhaps.

"The Naked Moon," the insect said at last.

Dante knew the place, a strip bar around the corner.

Maybe I am going mad, too, Dante thought. Maybe the insect is not here, and is just a voice in the plaster.

"When?"

He listened. The insect spoke.

"Now."

Then for a long time there was just the ticking noise, the faint clicking, and then after a little while that was gone, too.

PART TWO

FOUR

The Naked Moon sat on the far end of Broadway. An old-school joint, a rub-and-run parlor owned by the Orsini brothers, Gino and Carlo. The sidewalk sign promised local girls, neighborhood sweeties, though exactly what that meant anymore was hard to say, and the tattered pictures on the display board outside—women in aprons, college girls in cardigans, nurses, and schoolteachers—all looked as if they'd been posted decades before. Wholesome as hell if not for the uplifted apron, the naughty ruler, the fingers deep inside the elastic band.

Inside, the Moon was bone simple. Gino and some old Italians at the bar. A handful of tables. A stage with a velvet curtain and a pole in the middle. For years, the place had gotten by on the old routines, strictly hetero, but times had changed, and the old-fashioned grind didn't draw like it used to.

"It's a dead end," said Gino.

Gino's brother had had a stroke, and Gino ran the place alone now. On the other side of the counter hunched Old Man Pesci and his nephew Marinetti. Pesci was older than made any sense, wrinkled and ugly and bitter, barely able to get around—balanced precariously on the stool. His nephew, no young man himself, brought him here a couple nights a week, helping him downstairs from his apartment on Stockton, guiding him across the broken concrete.

"There's no future in anything," said Pesci.

"That's a bit extreme," said his nephew.

Gino, the owner, shook his head. He wore a mustache like a barber, dandered up with too much oil. "It's no-win. You put a girl up on the stage, you lose the fags. Go with the dancing fags, you lose the tourists."

"The Boom is doing okay."

Gino grunted.

The Boom was a competing institution just around the corner. There were a number of other grind shows struggling for an identity, but the Boom had gone techno, blending gays and straights in a live act, meanwhile streaming in an Internet simulcast from a sister club in Tokyo. The Boom was full of Asians, upscale businessmen, tourists, local hipsters with rings through their noses.

Gino, on the other hand, was a veteran of the old school, from back when San Francisco had been a shipyard town, from when all you had to do was throw out a big-breasted blonde in a sailor suit and the clientele would come in your hand.

"Things have changed."

"A man's a man, you ask me," said Pesci.

"My lease is almost up," said Gino. "I can't afford this place anymore."

"And a woman's a woman."

"On the Internet, everyone's the same. Man, woman— you can't even tell."

"Everyone's equal." Pesci said it with disdain. "It's perverted. What kind of man jacks off in front of a computer screen?"

"Foot traffic," said Gino. "Synergy. When Four X was on the corner—the mags up front, peeps in the back—you had people walking by. Nowadays . . ."

"It's not healthy, the way things are."

"All I know," said Gino, "sitting around the house like that, in one place too long, you get a hard-on. That's the nature of the human animal."

"I know." Pesci grinned through his yellow teeth. "I'm having that problem right now."

Onstage, one of the girls emerged from behind the velvet curtain. The music started. The old men glanced, leered, then lowered their noses to their drinks.

Dante had finished one drink and was nursing the second. Though the old Italians had never been quiet types, they were louder now that their numbers were diminishing.

Eyesight going. Hearing, too.

The older they got, the louder.

The crowd was sparse. Aside from the men at the bar, there was just a couple at a table in front of the stage, and another man sitting alone. His contact might be one of these. With the company, you could never tell their intentions. The voice on the phone had given no clue. *Just go to the Naked Moon. Someone will meet you.*

Though the girl was dancing, the conversation at the bar went on, local gossip. Stella's place was closing down apparently, the Serafina Café. Or that was the rumor. Stella was selling out to the Chinese, after all these years pushing meatballs and sauce across the red-checkered cloth.

"She sold out. Stella's husband, he would turn in his grave."

"I don't know. All those years, on her feet. He would be happy, maybe. She has money to retire," said Marinetti.

"You always take the other side."

"I am trying to find the bright side. The positive."

"There is no bright side. Stella's closing. This is the last place for us now."

"No more meatballs."

"No more wine."

"Just naked girls."

"You don't like it here?" said Gino. "It's not exactly good for business you know, your ugly faces at my bar."

Pesci scoffed. "You should be so lucky, to be so ugly as me," said Pesci. "Isn't that right?" He turned his attention to Dante at the end counter. "Your grandfather would be proud of you, that nose of yours."

"That's right," said Marinetti.

"True ugliness, it's a rare thing."

Marinetti agreed again. There was spittle on his chin.

"How's your cousin doing?" asked Pesci.

"Fine," said Dante.

"I bet he is."

From the tone of it, Pesci had heard the gossip, how his cousin was being investigated and heard, too, of the fuss out at Rossi's house. The old Italians knew everything, or acted like they did—and bad news, it gave them pleasure.

"That warehouse, it's a moneymaker. You're lucky your family got its hands on that."

His father and his uncle had picked it up because they were on the right side of things, because they had been friends with Mayor Rossi, back in the day, after World War II, when the waterfront was being divided up. There had been rumors back then, about how that was accomplished, but things had been simpler, more black and white, and in the end it didn't matter so much what you did as whose side you were on. The rumors had gotten nastier in the years since, about the kind of business that went down at Mancuso's warehouse. Those rumors, they were part of the reason he'd had to leave SFPD, pushed from the force, and ended up with the company.

"She's a little on the skinny side, wouldn't you say? That girl up there."

"That's the fashion," said Marinetti.

"I don't like it."

"Times change."

"Fuck the fashion."

"I think that's the idea."

When her act was done, the girl made the rounds. Dante knew the routine—from his old days working vice—and when she leaned over, he put a bill between her breasts. She dipped in a little closer, whispering into his ear.

She smiled. "I have one more show."

Pesci tilted toward Dante. The old man couldn't mind his business.

"You want her, she's available."

"Keep it down," said Gino.

Technically speaking, there was a no-mingle rule. You could buy the girl a drink, you could give her a tip, she could dance the air over your lap, but no touching. Those were the spoken rules. Unspoken, you gave the money to Gino, and she would meet you outside, and afterward, the two of you, you could do what you want.

"College girl." Pesci leered. It was what they always said about the girls, but of course, it was rarely true. "Working her way through. Maybe it's a little rough between you and what's her name, that girl up the hill. . . ." Pesci gave him a knowing glance, based on nothing, on rumor, on his intuitive ability to get under your skin. "A man needs a little outside fun."

"Sure," Dante said.

He hadn't come here for that, but let them think as they would.

FIVE

Dante sat by himself at one of the small tables at the back. The crowd had grown, but not by much. A tourist couple in matching Windbreakers, cameras about their necks. Three junior college kids, too young to be here, but with fake IDs good enough for Gino. Farther back, a solitary man, all by his lonesome, at a table in the shadows.

Dante had been through this before, back when he was with the company. They sent you someplace, and no one showed; then you got another call, another place to sit. In the meantime, you waited. It was the waiting that wore you down. During his years with the company, traveling, he'd developed certain habits, and just sitting here now, waiting, brought back the hunger associated with those habits. Amphetamines kept you up and other things helped you sleep and still, other, stronger things put you in a dream that made you feel as if you had escaped it all. Then you would wake up from the dream into some ugly bit of business that you didn't want to remember, and afterward the hunger would be sharper than before. He had indulged that hunger, more than once, dipping his long nose into the foil. It was a common malady in some lines of work.

Dante watched the show, the girls with their clumsy dances. Mostly, he'd worked homicide with the SFPD, but he'd spent some time with vice, too, and part of his job had been to frequent places like this, undercover. The place was full of violations. Some of the girls were underage, and the Vietnamese woman sat a little too long on Pesci's lap, and the solitary man in the back, glancing furtively at Dante, was rubbing his cock a little too vigorously by definition of city code.

But it was the kind of thing he would have ignored back then, searching for bigger fish, and which was none of his business now.

He watched the dancer.

She was some kind of mixed race. She had cocoa-colored skin, but her hair was blond. Dyed probably, but for some reason the color looked all right.

On the floor, she was artless and clumsy.

After she finished her number, she strolled up to him out of the blue smoke and whispered his name in his ear, tilting her head back, eyes clouded in an adolescent smokiness. She had too much sloppiness about her to be his contact, too much of the kid in her face. There were other ways she could have learned his name, from Gino at the bar maybe, who wanted him to hang around and buy watered-down drinks into the small hours of the night.

"I like your nose."

"How did you know my name?"

"Your friend told me."

"What friend?"

"It's a surprise."

"Man or woman?"

"Do you want to talk?"

"Not here."

"Make arrangements with Gino," she said, "and I'll meet you outside."

Dante walked to the far end of the counter, around the back side of the horseshoe. The drink window, it was called, though drinks were served by the waitress on the floor. It was the place where you paid off-the-record money. Gino didn't regard himself as a pimp. Payment was reimbursement for taking one of his girls off the floor. What arrangements you made with the girl, what you did, if money exchanged hands between you and her, how much, all that was your business.

Dante paid Gino and waited out front.

In a little while the girl came strutting through the side entrance on the parking lot. She was dressed in street clothes now, or something resembling them.

"Someone described me for you?"

"Your nose," she said.

The young woman wore a hip-length black vinyl jacket overtop a white skirt. She looked like a prostitute, but it was the style these days, especially among the young ones, drugged up on TV. This one was drugged up on something else. She had the sleepy look of a junkie, and it was there in her walk, and in the languid way she turned her head, the shine in the eyes. He'd seen it, too, while she danced. Could be she was older than she looked. That she was an agent after all. Half the people with the company were junked up, one way or the other, and he'd been down that path himself, unfolding the foil, eyes lowered, nose following the flame, chasing the smoke, the white tail of the dragon.

"A party," she said. "You're my date."

"What kind of party?"

"A small party. Just me and you. Your friends."

"Friends?"

She put her finger to her lips. "It's a surprise."

Dante felt something cold.

She shrugged.

He was tempted to shake it out of her.

"The room's been paid for," she said. "I have the key."

She took him up the way to a tourist hotel, the Sam Wong, a midrange place, not too plush, not too shabby— that had recently been bought up by one of the chains. The place had been called the Columbus Hotel once upon a time, and the visiting Italian opera stars had stayed here. According to the old stories, there had been tunnels underneath connecting it to the Chinese brothels, and the remnants of tunnels were still down there. Nowadays, it was tourists on a budget and businessmen like his cousin's new buddy, Dominick Greene, who stayed here—if indeed, Greene was what he pretended to be. Dante couldn't help his suspicion of the man.

There was a house phone on the wall near the elevator.

"What are you doing?"

"I thought I'd call. Let them know we're coming."

"I thought you had the key?"

"I do."

"Then there's no need, is there?"

The girl seemed hesitant. "I guess not."

"A surprise party, like you said."

They stepped into the elevator, and he sensed her nervousness and her youth. It occurred to him that she was exactly what she seemed. A girl alone in this elevator, this tight space. A young woman who had been through this kind of thing before, taking strange men up into hotel rooms, not knowing exactly what lay ahead, whether it would be a threesome, or two couples, or just a watcher, some guy going at her while the other got hot in the corner, just looking. Sometimes it was the other way around: Sometimes they wanted you to watch them.

Some hotels in the city, they had cameras to prevent molestations in the elevators, but not here. He leaned in toward the woman. She mistook his gesture and shifted in her skirt, as if he might want to lift it up.

"You can touch me if you want."

"Who sent you?"

"No names."

"A man or a woman?"

"A surprise," she said. "Remember?"

"You said friends. . . . There was more than one?"

The way she looked at him, he saw that she thought this

maybe was part of the foreplay, that it got him excited, talking about this kind of thing.

"I was told you would be like this. That you would want to know everything."

The elevator had arrived, but he didn't let her out. He pushed her up against the controls, not too hard but hard enough. She misinterpreted the motion anyway and touched him down low.

"Describe him," Dante said.

"Him?"

"Or her. If that's the way it was."

"Who said it was just one?"

"How many?"

"You're kinky."

"How many?" he repeated. He pushed her hand away, grabbing her more roughly now. The girl's eyes widened, and he saw the flicker of panic.

"As many as you want. A man alone. A woman. Three, five . . . What the fuck do you want?"

What he did next, maybe it was magnanimous. Because he suspected this girl did not know what was going on and there was no sense getting her involved. Or because he was getting aroused in a way that had some ugliness to it, and he did not want to walk that line. Or because deep down, he knew it didn't matter. Whoever had set this up with her, however many, he would find out in a minute, as soon as he walked into that room.

"Go downstairs," he said.

"Three hundred," she said. "I was promised three hundred."

"I paid Gino."

"The money you gave Gino is for Gino. I need mine."

"I don't have that much."

He gave her a half-dozen twenties. The young woman took the money and put it in her purse. It was not a rushed gesture, but slow, even delicate. He thought of Marilyn, with David Lake, in the seven-hundred-count Egyptian-cotton sheets, down there in Santa Barbara, with the olive trees in the hills under the coastal sun. The girl glanced back up at him, subdued, the lips full, chin down but eyes up. She clicked the purse, stepping closer as she did so, brushing against him, and he could see, by the turn of the lips, that she regarded him as a fool, paying for something he wasn't going to get. That part of her had also liked the rough treatment.

"Go."

"This wasn't the agreement. It was three hundred."

"That's all I have with me. Give me your address. I'll give you the rest tomorrow."

"No, you won't."

"Call the cops, if you have a problem. Or I can just call the front desk."

She twisted her lips, surly as hell, then changed her manner altogether, wondering if he was one of those, the kind of customer who would pay even if he didn't want to fuck.

"You can find me at Gino's," she said. "You want to do this again."

"Wait a minute."

"What?"

"The room key."

Dante waited until the girl was in the elevator, then went down the hall. He still didn't know about her. His old friends at the company were insidious with their games. His guess, she was no agent, just a pony, as the expression went, someone the agent had given a few dollars to carry him in. It was possible he was wrong, but he didn't think so. Most likely, she was out on the street with her money, headed not for Gino's but toward some street corner where she could get more powder. He'd seen how it went, during his days with vice. If she couldn't find anything close by, there was a twenty-four-hour gallery down under the freeway, the other side of Market. The girls with hard habits, they sold themselves on the street corner across from the freeway, keeping everything convenient. For a moment, despite himself, he was tempted to go with her.

Instead he slid the magnetic card into the lock and pushed open the door.

The room was dark. There was no one inside.

The sheets had been turned down, a couple of chocolates on the pillows, but there was no sign that anyone had been around.

He went to the window and looked down eight stories to the sidewalk below, the figures moving through the yellow light, down Broadway, into Chinatown, up the long hill toward Coit Tower.

He sat on the edge of the bed. He called downstairs to find out the name under which the room had been registered.

Smith.

Original, he thought.

He could wait here, see if anyone showed, but it seemed the whole thing had been some kind of game. A distraction. Why?

He left quickly then, descending, joining the figures in the yellow light below, only it didn't seem yellow once you were in it. He hurried toward Union. It was late, and the tourists were outnumbered by the vagabonds. A couple staggered hand in hand, Midwesterners in love with the city. Meanwhile a handful of Asian kids watched from the shadows—not good kids, Dante could see in a glance—but the couple was oblivious. A cop drove by, but he was oblivious, too. If I were a better man, Dante thought, I might simply stand here until the couple walked safely by. Diffuse the moment, deterring what might be coming by his simple presence—a robbery, a mugging, or worse. Instead he headed around the corner, up toward Marilyn.

There had been a threat implicit in that voice, in that static, and he knew how the company operated.

Marilyn's apartment was at the top of Union—in a corner Victorian. The place was on a rise, up off the street, but before he could climb the stairs, he saw the Mercedes in the driveway. Though the front of the apartment lay in darkness, a light issued from the back, from the bedroom.

He glanced at the Mercedes and then back at her window. He took the cell out of his pocket.

She had an old-fashioned phone in the bedroom, a landline without a call screen. He had urged her to replace it, so she could identify incoming callers, but she'd paid no attention.

"Hello."

Her voice was husky, as if she had just woken from sleep. In the background, he could hear someone else, a man's voice.

He clicked off.

He had been mistaken, his worries unfounded. Marilyn was safe, at least for the time being. The Mercedes belonged to David Lake.

SIX

Fresno Street was not a street at all, but an alley, wider than the alleys in Chinatown, true, but an alley nonetheless: two blocks of row houses, with a tavern at one end, down there in the bottom of the gulley, and an apartment building at the top of the rise. Though the sky was black and moonless, the alley was filled with shadows. Yellow light issued from the barred windows of the homes, through the fire escapes, and the railed shadows fell upon the street.

In the blackness of the alley, his father's house had the look of a place abandoned. No curtains, only blinds, and these cantilevered in such a way that the glass seemed to absorb the darkness, suggesting a greater emptiness within.

He had left the front light on inside the house, he was all but sure, but it was off now. Perhaps he was mistaken, but he did not take the chance. He dropped through a casement window into the garage. It hadn't been there originally, the garage. His father had had it placed beneath, at considerable expense, dug out into the slope beneath the foundation.

Dante stood listening.

The house creaked, a door slammed, but the houses were close here, the walls thin, and the slamming could have come from anywhere nearby.

The garage had a six-foot ceiling. It was below grade, dark in the daytime, but he nonetheless could make out the shapes of the boxes around him. He felt a draft and noticed a softness in the darkness ahead, a graying at the top of the basement stairs. The kitchen door at the top of those stairs had been left open. He edged forward. Papers underfoot, clothing, knickknacks, and family miscellany. Boxes opened, strewn and scattered.

He stood in the doorway for a long time. The one advantage Dante had, he knew the place well. He knew every floorboard, every creak. Once he would have proceeded differently, furrowing his way from room to room, searching. Instead, now, he moved once and once only, stepping swiftly across the threshold, quietly, gun in hand, across the open space into the kitchen. He sat in one of the chairs at the table. From here, he could see both the living room—with the front door—and the landing stairs descending past the kitchen to the courtyard below. These were the only ways out.

Now he sat and listened some more.

To the creaking. The shifting and sighing of the house. The surge of the furnace and voices from one of the apartments in the building beyond. It all mingled, and he sat in the darkness, not moving, just listening. Sitting like a man asleep. He had grown up in this house, and he knew how the imagination transformed the creaking into footfalls, how a window shutting next door, a laugh in the street, traveled through the walls, how it could make you jump. He knew, too, how the sounds infiltrated your dreams. After a while, he concluded the intruder had left, likely before he himself had arrived, but he kept still nonetheless, and in the stillness, maybe he did sleep. He heard the fluttering of wings—an explosion of birdsong out in the alley, parrots in the euca-lyptus. The light turned gray, and he saw himself as if in a dream, moving through that grayness, groping, room to room, swiveling, gun in hand. The house had been ran-sacked. Clothes scattered. Cushions split. Drawers upturned and emptied.

The routine with the prostitute—the cat and the mouse—it had all been a distraction, to keep him out of the house. Whatever they had been looking for, they hadn't found it, he knew, because there was nothing here to find.

His guess, his visitor had known that as well.

It was all gesture—a way of letting him know his time was up.

He knew what they wanted, though. He knew what this was about. Three years ago, he had returned to San Francisco on assignment with the company. He'd wanted out, and that last assignment had provided a way. Part of that assignment had involved retrieving the journal of Ru Shen, a deceased businessman, an evangelical Chinese, a charismatic figure of sorts, with ties on both sides of the Pacific, a man of principle, it was said, with access to sensitive information, who'd betrayed those principles, depending on your point of view: not just an agent, but a double agent, he'd kept a detailed record that jeopardized the secret workings of the company, the covert operations linking the official intelligence operation to the unofficial, the criminal to the governmental. The short of it was that Ru Shen had been murdered and the journal destroyed, but Dante did not tell the company this latter fact. Rather, he had allowed them to think that the journal still existed, and he had used its alleged existence to reach a kind of stasis, buying his own way out of the company, so to speak, with the threat of revealing whatever information was inside. In the event of his death, all would be revealed. It was a dangerous game, one that could come undone at any time, and for this reason, and for the safety of those around him, Dante had not intended to stay in San Francisco but rather to disappear, to abandon his identity. But there was Marilyn. There was this house. One day had passed, then another, and though he'd feared this would come, he'd let himself think his bluff had worked these last three years. Now the company claimed someone was leaking their secrets. So far as he knew, there was only one other person in the city who knew about Ru Shen's journal. The man was a friend of his father's, Joe Rossi, the former mayor whose youngest daughter, Gennae, was running for mayor now.

SEVEN

Dante went down to the warehouse first, but Gary was not there, and so he climbed the hill to the top of Telegraph. Gary lived in a big house, ungainly, terraced into the rock, huge windows on every tier, tinted so you could see out but not in—and the tint gave the windows on odd metallic sheen. Gary had wired the place for security: cameras everywhere, laser-triggered switches, video monitors inside and out. The system was too sensitive, though, set off by raccoons on the front lawn, birds on the wing, falling shadows. As a result, the system was disabled much of the time—though it was true also that Gary sat for hours at the video monitors, watching the front lawn on the black-and-white screen.

No one answered the front door.

Dante walked around the back. His cousin stood on the second-story balcony, looking down.

"You're not answering the door these days?"

"I could see you on the monitor."

"Are you going to let me up?"

"I am thinking about it."

"You were the one who called me."

"Three times," his cousin said. "Three times, I called you."

His cousin hit the switch and Dante climbed the stairs. Ten years ago, the property had belonged to a bachelor who'd worked down at the Mancuso warehouse—a straggle of anise weeds and rocks with a cabin that faced away from the view. Gary had torn the cabin down and dozed the land, jackhammering the bedrock, terracing in a house that sprawled over the lot, a jumble of vaulted archways and inlaid floors, balconies and marble counters, a whirl tub built into the deck and security cameras mounted underneath the eaves.

"So you decided to come after all."

"I expected to find you at the warehouse."

"I have a situation."

"So I've heard."

"An auditor. He was coming in this morning. So I decided not to be there."

"The books aren't there?"

"They can't audit what they can't see."

"That will work only so long."

They both knew what had been going on at the warehouse and had been going on for years. Shipments in, off ledger. Shipments out in the middle of the night. Underneath-the-table money. No questions asked. The Mancuso warehouse was one of the few still operating on the San Francisco side. The port business had moved over to Oakland—where the bay was regularly dredged—and it was through other arrangements that the business kept going.

The warehouse had been under investigation before. In the end, these investigations always faltered, but this one was being headed up by a woman from SI, a Chinese cop by the name of Leanora Chin. Dante knew her from his time on the force.

The Lady in Blue, so called.

This was how her fellow cops referred to her, on account, no matter the occasion, she always had the look of someone in uniform. She always wore the same blunt cut. Her clothes, it seemed, were always blue.

"I didn't start this mess," Gary said. "I inherited it."

Inside the living room, smooth surfaces were everywhere, hard and sleek, Italian furniture, glass and gold leaf, all contemporary, expensive, colors bright and simple. There was a carton upturned on the glass table. A shattered bottle of wine. A broken vase on the floor.

"Viola had one of her fits," he said.

Dante knew about Viola's fits. He had seen her once sweep a shelf of imported crystal from the display. He'd seen her go after Gary and rip his shirtfront with her long nails. He'd seen her inflamed, and he'd heard her wail. In the dining nook, a china plate lay shattered, a designer piece, some rococo nonsense, and there was a great red smear on the wall. Tomato sauce.

Viola was a wild one, but Gary was no prince.

"Where is she?"

"Tahoe . . ." He pointed. "I'm not cleaning it up. It's her mess."

"Is she coming back?"

"She always comes back," he said ruefully.

It was true: Viola always came back. Or she always had in the past. She liked the house with its big windows and her closet full of clothes and the jet-black Jaguar in the garage. Nonetheless, she was the third wife, and she had her reasons to explode. A slew of stepkids in and out. Gary mooning over his first wife, fighting with the second. Sleeping with Lola down at the warehouse, bending her over the big metal desk. Not to mention the money problems now, the whole thing a house of cards. With the Feds standing outside, ready to blow it all over.

"She's talking to lawyers. She's going to testify against me if I don't give her everything I own."

"She'll calm down."

"She's jealous. She thinks there's another woman."

"Another one?"

"It was business, I tried to explain. With the woman— and her husband." Gary smirked despite himself, forever proud of his dalliances, though his eyes held a self-conscious glimmer that Dante had seen often enough, along with a hint of fear. It could be difficult to tell when his cousin was lying.

"What kind of business?"

"This is your fault, too," Gary said.

"I don't have anything to do with the warehouse."

"No, of course not. You're too good for that."

By stipulation of the will, Dante remained half owner. He had given the day-to-day operations over to his cousin years ago, in return for a percentage. In actuality, the business had not turned a profit in years, at least not on paper, and the property was mortgaged beyond its value. Dante had put a second mortgage on the place out on Fresno, to help his cousin out, but that, too, was sliding toward arrears.

"You always thought you deserved it all," Gary said. "But the truth is, you don't deserve anything. I am not even blood. I never wanted it. They came over to Italy and dragged me here. They dressed me up."

Gary spread his arms wide in a beseeching gesture. Dante had seen the gesture before and he had heard the argument, too. His adopted cousin had used the argument ever since he was a kid, every time he got in over his head. If Salvatore and Regina Mancuso had left him in the orphanage, if they had not adopted him, none of this would ever have happened.

"Do you think I wanted this life?"

"It doesn't matter. You've got it."

"I didn't want this."

But his cousin had wanted it. Or he had wanted the stuff, anyway. He liked his sports car and his glass tile bathroom and his ten-jet Jacuzzi. He loved his house that looked out over the whole world and his video-monitoring system that let him see every bug crawling up the walk. He loved it even now, angry as he was. Loved catching sight of himself in the big gilt mirror, here in the living room, hands on his hips, staring back at himself in his silk shirt, his white slacks and his loafers with the tassels, his gold Rolex.

But it wasn't enough.

Dante's uncle had given Gary everything he could, but now the old ones were dead and Gary had run up against the wall.

Because it wasn't Gary who ran the warehouse anymore. It was the Wus. He was their front, their shill. He was really nothing more than a paid fall guy—one who wasn't particularly discreet—and it was a wonder they hadn't gotten rid of him a long time ago.

All Gary'd had to do was close his eyes and take the money, but his cousin had bungled the laundering operations. He'd also gotten himself into debt.

"The Wus are tied in with the CIA, you know. They can do any goddamn thing they want."

His cousin looked at him pointedly. It was a common rumor, containing a degree of truth. Dante didn't argue.

"This guy Dominick Greene. Who is he?"

"No one. Just some two-bit. I drank with him a couple of times, that's all."

"What does he want?"

"He works for a fabric wholesaler. Merchandise—needs expedited delivery."

"You should be careful."

"This isn't about him." His cousin's jaw tightened, and then the eyes went dark, woeful. "I need your help."

"I don't have money," Dante said.

"It's not cash," Gary said, irritated, though Dante knew his cousin was perennially short of money. "I talked to some people. . . . If you help them, if you cooperate," he said, "they'll help me. They have insider contacts. They'll kill the investigation."

Dante thought of Greene again. He thought of the call he himself had received, the insect down there in its den.

"Someone's pulling your leg," he said.

"This isn't just for me. I've got two ex-wives . . . kids . . . responsibilities." Gary hung his head. "This cop, Chin—with Special Investigations—she's been after the Wus for years. Meantime, she's got me in a bind."

Dante knew his cousin's dilemma. Leanora Chin wanted the Wu operation and would use his cousin to get it. Other investigators had gone after the Wus before, cops tougher on the surface, but these others had either been bought off or disappeared. Meanwhile Chin had threatened to get the IRS on his cousin if he didn't reveal the inner operations. She had offered him immunity if he cooperated, but if Gary took her offer, the Wus would come after him. His cousin's only way out, if he wanted to avoid jail time on one side and the Wus on the other, was to join Witness Protection. Gary didn't want to do that. He didn't want to leave everything behind.

"What makes you think I can do anything?" asked Dante.

"I got a call, a visit . . . from some people. . . ."

"What people?"

"All you have to do, is give them what they want."

His looks curled in an expression Dante remembered from their boyhood. When his cousin was desperate, he did foolish things. He grabbed at straws. He looked around for someone to blame, to pull down with him. Nevertheless, his cousin knew a lot, from his years at the trade—about the Wus, about this and that—and as Dante studied his cousin's face, he wondered if his cousin had stumbled upon something else.

"What were you doing at Rossi's?"

"Just paying my respects."

"That's not what I heard."

"People exaggerate."

"There was a scene."

"Big friend of the family, that one. Mayor for twelve years. I asked him to use his influence, that's all. To get this cop off my back. But fuck me, that's his attitude. Fuck me."

"He's not mayor anymore."

"I wouldn't have gone out there if you'd answered my goddamn calls."

"What do you expect me to do?"

"You can help. That's what I was told."

"Who told you that?"

His cousin shook his head. "I was told in confidence."

"Greene?"

His cousin turned away. Gary was weak—and if he went after him, if he pushed him hard enough, his cousin might tell him—but Dante felt the same hesitation he'd felt with the girl from Gino's, who'd led him to the hotel room. It was sometimes better to let the messenger be, to let the pony go. Force Gary to talk, drag him in too far, there might be repercussions he could not see. He thought of Marilyn. He'd lingered in town too long, the company knew his every vulnerability, and now it was too late to leave.

"It was a friendly visit. Like I said, if you help them," he said, "they'll help us. We can save the business."

"I don't know what you're talking about."

"You're lying."

"No." Dante dropped his voice, looking his cousin in the eye. They'd been raised like brothers, two kids on the block, and he saw his cousin hesitating under his glance, guilty, sheepish. But his cousin was right: Dante was not telling him everything.

"You're supposed to be the good one," said Gary. "The cop . . . but it turns out, you're the one with all the nasty friends."

His cousin sat on the couch, shoulders bent, hands clasped between his knees. He had dark brown eyes, curly hair, boyish. The women had always liked him, even those who saw through him. You could see the softness in him, something about to relent, the desire to be good—but in the end, he was always looking for another way. He got up now, smiling that kid smile, and went to the bookcase. There were pictures up there. Dante's own father and mother. Himself and his cousin on the stoop.

"Remember?" his cousin asked.

"Yeah."

"There's more pictures."

"I know."

"The old days."

More pictures, the two of them together. Of Uncle Salvatore and Aunt Regina. More cousins, more family. Old
fishermen on the dock. His cousin gave him the soft look.
"I miss them."

"Yeah."

"It seems like just a minute ago, they were all here. In
another minute, us, too, we'll be gone also."

"Time passes."

"There's no such thing as time—remember. That's what
the priest used to say, the nuns. It's just one moment. The
big forever."

"I remember."

"So you think about it—we're already dead."

"Not quite."

"This is your fault, too. If you had come into the business," he said. "If you had done what your father wanted,
things wouldn't be this way."

It was a perverse logic, typical of his cousin, but there
was an element of truth. If he had gone into the business,
if he had taken charge—if he had married Marilyn, years
ago—if he'd never gone to New Orleans, then his friends
at the company would never have paid his cousin a visit,
in whatever outfit, whatever guise, promising to pull the
strings that would kill the investigation and make everything
right.

His cousin looked at him now, his eyes soft and earnest, the little boy on the street, on the stoop, in the foreign country, in over his head.

"Just give them what they want," Gary said.

PART THREE

EIGHT

A chicken could not cluck in Portsmouth Square, a fish could not whisper, without the sound carrying into the chambers of Love Wu, atop the Empress Building. Or this was the saying of the old men playing mah-jongg on the stone benches in the square.

The Empress was not on the square itself, but on the rise, a block back, and the sound carried to the upper stories. The building was not in itself impressive, seven stories high, built with brick, then covered with deteriorating stucco on the upper layers. At the top it had been corniced in the fashion of a pagoda, though this facade, too, was in partial disrepair.

On the street level, the building housed the ubiquitous vegetable parlors and junk palaces of Chinatown, stalls crammed with cheap luggage and cheaper produce. Above that stood the offices of the Wu Benevolent Association—and on the top floor, or so it was said, the chambers of Love Wu himself.

Love Wu, the perverse, the ancient one, ruler of the hidden kingdom.

Father of Chinatown, to whom the wind carried every sound. Founder of the Wu Benevolent Association, the oldest of the Chinese associations.

You could not breathe, you could not whisper, without Love Wu knowing.

The benevolent associations were old institutions in Chinatown, offering help to newcomers, aid to the indigent, business ties. Older still were the tongs: secret societies with their roots in the Chinese underworld. The lines between the tongs and the associations were not always clear, even now. Both went back to the time when the Chinese clipper ships had anchored by night in the fog off the Golden Gate, and the smugglers brought their longboats up to the wharf in the small hours, carrying cargo for the opium dens, women for the brothels. They brought indentured labor for the railroads, to hoe the fields and clean the toilets. Men to dig the basement tunnels that extended beneath Chinatown and spiraled out into the city. But the contraband had gone both ways. If a local strayed too close to the wharf at night, stood too long on a street corner, that person—man, woman or child—might find themselves bound and gagged, facedown in a Chinese longboat. Headed out to those clippers in the fog.

A white slave.

A galley mate for life. A concubine. A child for the delight of Oriental perversions.

Love Wu had been around since the time of the tunnels, it was said, though that would make him impossibly old. The stories about him were contradictory, his birth date a matter of conjecture. The streets were full of his relations—sons, nieces, granddaughters, cousins. But as these relations grew old and passed into the grave, Love Wu remained.

No.

He had died long ago. He was not one man, but many. In fact, Love Wu was not a man at all but a title given to a man: a designation passed along from one dying kinsman to the next.

No.

Love Wu had not died. Rather he had returned to China. He lived in a monastery in Sonoma. He was the old beggar you saw every day on the corner, wandering the streets in disguise.

No.

He still lived on the top floor of the Empress Building, in the upper story, above the manifold operations of the Wu Benevolent Association. His chambers opened onto the balcony at the top of the building, and sometimes at night his shadow could be seen moving in the yellow light that issued from those slatted doors.

He dwelled in his library there, among the ancient scrolls, listening to the secrets drift up from the street. There were stories about his library, and the information recorded there.

Dante had seen him once, years ago. Or rather he had heard the name, Love Wu, issue through the crowd, and seen an old Chinaman in silk garments and braided hair being escorted across the street like some dignitary.

Back hunched, infirm.

The Italians joked, every old man in Chinatown. There goes Love Wu.

It was impossible he could still be alive.

Regardless, the smuggling continued. Not just laborers, tucked in the hold of a ship. Not just AK-47s and counterfeit cell phones, heroin and cocaine, black market computers and AAA batteries, factory defective goods recycled in new wrapping. Information, too, trade secrets from Silicon Valley, under-the-counter real estate deals, money to launder. And the news of these dealings carried upward to the old man forever on the verge of death. A man who was not a man at all but a sunken spot on the bed—ashes in an urn—dust scattered over the ocean.

Everything got back to him, sooner or later.

He had a million spies.

Hotel clerks. Fishmongers. Maids.

Attorneys and cops.

Scribes.

As a child, restless in his bed on Fresno Street, listening to the creaking of the old house, Dante had imagined what it was like to be Love Wu, hearing what he heard, decoding the secret language—and sometimes, on the edge of sleep, it seemed he actually understood. Dante had the same sensation now, leaving his cousin's house, midstep—as if he were looking down on himself from up there, listening to the breeze on the other side of those slatted doors.

Ru Shen.

NINE

It was election season, and overnight a new wave of campaign flyers had been plastered along Kearny: on the telephone poles and bus shelters, on the plywood sheeting under the construction overhangs. Identical pictures of Gennae Rossi, placed one after another. Daughter of Joe Rossi, the former mayor. Dark horse candidate for mayor now, sentimental favorite in North Beach. Running against Ching Lee on one side, and the incumbent Edwards on the other. Whoever posted them had continued past Columbus, around the corner into Chinatown, but here the likenesses had already been defaced. The same was true on the other side of Columbus, however. Lee's posters did not last long before they were peeled and plastered over with Gennae Rossi's face.

Above the battle, in the higher reaches—on the billboards, on the sides of buildings—laminated on the panels of a passing bus—was the image of the incumbent: Dale Edwards.

Edwards had more money than the others, more campaign funds, and there were questions in the paper about where the money came from, but in one way, it did not matter. His face, too, was scrawled with graffiti.

Dante was on his way to find the girl from the other night. He'd been to Gino's earlier, but she'd missed her shift, so he got her address from one of the other girls. He had not pushed her that night in the elevator, but told himself, now, with some cash on the table, she might describe for him the person or persons who had sent her his way. He could push her in ways he could not push his cousin—and without the same kind of repercussions. Then pack her on the bus and send her back to from wherever she came.

It would be the best thing, the safest all around.

As Dante turned the corner, down into the flats, there were fewer posters. This was where the dancer lived, Gino's girl—in one of the brick apartments that survived in the shadows of the high-rises along the Embarcadero. It was all blacktop and concrete here, parking garages and steel gates. It had been marsh once—smelling of sulfur and septic—and it still smelled that way. The ground sumped, and the drains backed up, and the stench rose through the gratings of the corner sewers.

The girl lived in a three-story walk-up that was slated to be torn down, but she did not answer the door. After a while the manager appeared and told Dante he had not seen her for several days.

"Where did she go?"

"I don't know. She's by the week."

"She moved out?"

"You a cop?"

"No."

"What do you want with her, then?"

"I'm a friend."

"I told her, none of that kind of business here."

"It's not that way."

"She's by the week," he said again. "She's got two more days. But I haven't seen her."

"Does she have a forwarding?"

The man laughed. "What kind of place do you think this is?"

Dante left. He went up through Chinatown into Portsmouth Square. On the causeway leading down from the Chinese Cultural Center, some workers were in the final stages of dismantling an exhibit, "Across the Water," that had been financed by the Wu Benevolent Association. There had been some controversy, he remembered, regarding some artifacts that the association had taken and placed in its private collection, in the Empress Building across the way.

Dante wondered where the girl had gone.

It did not mean anything. Girls like her, they came and went all the time. The city was like that. He wondered if he'd made a mistake—not getting to the girl when he could.

He tried to reach Marilyn at Prospero's, but there was no answer.

Out with clients, according to the receptionist.

Some couple, new in town.

Marilyn had been dragging them all over.

TEN

There was no reason anymore to go to the Serafina Café. It had been lively once, cops at the lunch counter and the tables full of families, old men with napkins tucked into their shirtfronts, the place full of noise, half-drunk bohos, and a card game in the back, kids spilling sauce on their Sunday best, men flirting with their brothers' wives. Stella scolding her husband in the kitchen while the regulars laughed and wept and George Marinetti announced his daughter's wedding at the bar. They were dead now, most of them, and their children moved away, and the place was too dark for the tourists, too full of dust. The food was not what it used to be, and it was just the oldest of the old, coming for the gossip and the wine, but the wine was better elsewhere, and cheaper, and so now it was just the photos along the bar and the dead ones gossiping in the shadows. There was no reason to come here, but Dante came anyway.

An old habit, inherited from his father. Come to listen to the dead. To hang his long nose over the bar.

Inside, the restaurant was all but empty. It was only Stella Lamantia, the owner, and the blind woman Julia Besozi, who sat as she always sat, dressed primly, perfectly erect, with her legs crossed and one shoulder toward the window. The TV played in the corner. Julia could not see, but her hearing was fine.

Stella meanwhile had out her broom and made a show of sweeping the place, pushing the dust toward the corner. This was not usual. Usually, Stella had a Chinaman who did the sweeping and washed the dishes, but the man was nowhere in sight. What Pesci and his nephew had told him the other night, over at Gino's, was true enough.

Stella was closing the place down.

"All I have is spaghetti."

"All right."

"It's cold."

"Okay."

"And the bread is hard."

When Stella came back with the food, it was in the condition as promised.

"I would make it fresh," she said, though her voice carried no hint of apology, "but this one, that one over there"—she pointed toward the Widow Besozi—"she eats nothing. And if it's just one person, why cook?"

"I like it cold," said Dante.

"Of course you do," she said. "You never had any sense."

"Pesci is mad, for her closing," said Besozi. "You know how he is. Leads that nephew around like some goat."

"They boycott me, that's what they are doing. Thirty years, forty years, I can't tell you how long, that man has been coming in here, filling the air with his stinking cigarettes—and this is my thanks."

Julia Besozi let out a small moan.

"Look," said Besozi. "It's Gennae Rossi."

On the television, Gennae Rossi filled the screen, the darling of North Beach, dark haired and olive skinned. The volume was low. Besozi might not be able to see, but her hearing was sharp. The old woman's posture came yet more erect. Everyone knew Gennae Rossi's story. The mayor's daughter, a wholesome girl with a streak of compassion, who every Saturday served up chow for the old ones down at Fugazi Hall. A few years back, she'd come down with multiple sclerosis, not the worst strain of the disease, but bad enough. She took the podium standing, sometimes, but wheeled the streets in her chair. Nonetheless, she'd gotten herself on the city council, and now she was running for mayor. Though she was a long-shot candidate, behind both Edwards and Lee in the polls, her presence rankled the race. A cult of sorts had developed around her, an odd coalition. Old women from the Beach. Hipsters from the Mission. The shops sold necklaces of her image hung on string.

"I have a lock of her hair," said Besozi.

"It's not her hair."

"Yes, it is."

"Keep it in your purse."

"Why?"

"It's not real."

"No. It's beautiful."

"She has a hook nose."

"You sound like Pesci," said Besozi. "He's an awful man. He's losing his mind."

Stella glanced toward the screen. At the moment, on the television, Gennae Rossi worked the sidewalk in front of the building that had burned on account of the hydrants that had failed. It was a big issue, the sporadic water pressure all over the Beach. City crews had been busy down on Columbus forever it seemed, tearing up asphalt, searching for the broken main.

"The woman's an opportunist," said Stella. "Just like her father."

Stella stood lamenting her situation. She had signed her lease over to the owners of the Chinese disco next door, who planned on punching a whole in the wall, expanding into her old space. The fault for this went back to Rossi thirty years ago, who had sold the city out to the Chinese. It was a tangled logic, but Dante understood. He had heard it from a hundred others who, like Stella, had vowed never to sell.

"I got good money, though," said Stella. "I didn't just sign it over. I got mine."

The old Italians always said this.

Dante ate. Besozi leaned against the wall. Stella swept.

The television showed the Chinese candidate now, his

rally truck, then Edwards, the incumbent, working the outer Richmond, out in the sand dunes, among the new middle class, trying to wrestle for himself some of the Asian vote.

While he was eating, Marilyn returned his call. Stella did not like people talking on a cell in her place. It was unnatural. It made her ill just to see someone, head over their food, talking to someone she could not see. Sometimes, such situations, she cleared your plate early and took away your wine.

"No telephones at the table."

Dante wrapped his fingers around the stemware and batted the old woman away.

"No," he said.

"What?" said Marilyn.

"Are you all right?" he asked.

"Of course. I've been with clients all morning."

"Give me that glass," said Stella. "Everyone in your family, they are difficult. I heard about your cousin, out at Rossi's. What was that about anyway? What's the matter with him?"

Dante let the glass go.

Stella's son had appeared in the back of the restaurant, a thick-shouldered man, a few years older than Dante, graying at the temples with a bald spot in back.

"Stop it, Mom," he said.

"What's this about?" asked Marilyn.

On her end, there was noise in the background, suggesting another restaurant—the sound of dishware, glasses clattering, laughter. A place more lively, in some ways, than Stella's. Marilyn's voice was cheerful, but distant. At the same time, Dante felt the noose tightening. The longer he stayed in North Beach, the more he risked drawing them to her. Then there was the matter of David Lake.

"I need to see you," he said.

"Okay."

"Angel Island," he said. "Do you still want to go?"

"Saturday?"

"That will be too late. The buyer, he's taking the boat."

"Let me see."

She put the phone on mute. Along the counter where Dante sat, there were pictures embedded under the glass, old-timers, people from the neighborhood. When Marilyn came back, the sound was different, as if she had stepped into another, quieter world, as if, somehow, she were speaking to him from the world under the glass counter. In one of those pictures, Dante's father was standing with Joe Rossi, holding a giant fish by a string.

"Yes," Marilyn said. Her voice was soft, intimate. "Tomorrow."

Out back, Stella and her son were taking stuff out of his pickup, loading it onto one of those sidewalk lifts that rose from under the metal grating in the alley: the type used to take produce into the basement beneath the restaurant.

Only Stella and her son were loading the lift with old furniture and household junk.

"It's been in my garage for years," said Stella. "We put it here, it's for the new owner. It's their problem, not ours."

"Saves a trip to the dump," said the son.

"We have no choice but to sell."

"No."

"Johnny Pesci, he doesn't like it, for all I care, he can shoot himself in the head."

"Pecsi would sell, too," said her boy, "if he had anything to sell."

Stella did not take a meek posture. She stood as she often stood, hands on her hips, breasts out, watching the stuff get lowered down, pleased to be getting rid of it this way, dumping it on the new owners, taking their money, giving herself the last laugh.

"Another thing they don't know, these people. The lock to the back door is broken," said Stella. "It's been broken for years. All you have to do is push down, a certain way." Dante remembered how in the old days, people would come back after hours, play poker at the back tables. "But do you think I am going to tell them? What do I care, some punk comes in and trashes the place. It's not my problem now."

Dante helped Stella's son unload the stuff, pushing it against the wall down below. Supposedly, the basements here had been part of a tunnel system once, built by the Chinese, and the Italians had used the tunnels during Prohibition. Perhaps it was true. Beneath the concrete, there appeared to be the outlines of a door that had been cemented over, but it was hard to be sure. Dante rode the lift up and stood with Stella out in the alley. He needed to go see Rossi, to find out what had gone on with his cousin, what the fuss had been about, but according to the television, Rossi was on the campaign trail with his daughter—and would introduce her at a dinner event later this evening. Dante doubted the old man would be at his house on Russian Hill.

"My lunch, I have to pay," said Dante.

"It's my last day," said Stella.

"Does that mean I get a discount?"

"No," she said. "I charge double."

She balled up her apron and threw it in the corner, next to the broom. The sink was full of dishes. "You should marry that girl," Stella told him. "You should marry her and get out." Then she brought Julia Besozi another glass of port.

ELEVEN

An unmarked car sat at the bottom of Fresno Street, and a man with blond hair lingered behind the wheel. He was a thick-necked man, whom Dante had never seen before—but the man gave Dante the hard once-over and hopped on his cell. Dante kept walking. When he was halfway up the block, two figures appeared at the top of the hill, approaching him, and he heard the car door open behind him.

He recognized the two figures at the crest of the street. One was Frank Angelo, whom Dante had worked with years ago, when Dante himself had been on the force. The other was the cop his cousin had mentioned, Leanora Chin, from Special Investigations. As it happened, she did not wear blue, but gray: a Chinese woman in a dark blouse and pencil skirt. The effect was pretty much the same.

"Mancuso."

Angelo called the name pleasantly, or pleasantly enough.

They had been friends once, partners on the beat. Dante stopped in the middle of the road. The three cops kept coming, forming a triangle around him, with Angelo and Chin in front, and the big blond man anchoring the apex behind.

"Déjà vu," said Angelo.

It was an expression from the old days, when he and Angelo had worked homicide together, a phrase they used when they came across a familiar mug in the book, an old face associated with a new crime. Angelo had the appearance of a reasonable man, which was part of the reason he had moved up the department ladder, at least for a while. His smile, though, turned a little too much at the corners, knifelike, a sideways gash.

"You didn't recognize me?"

"What is it?"

"No hello? No friendly wave?"

"I didn't want to interrupt your stroll."

"How do you think that makes me feel, you ignore me like that?"

"What do you want?"

"You're a bitter soul," said Angelo. He said it in a friendly way, almost joking, like a brother who liked to bicker. Chin, on the other hand, was a delicate-boned woman with high cheeks and gray eyes. Dante had encountered her before, and knew she did not go in for this kind of banter. She was heading the investigation into his cousin, so he wasn't surprised to see her. Angelo's presence was a bit harder to figure.

"Could we get off the street, Mr. Mancuso?" said Chin. "We'd like to talk with you."

"Yes. How about we step inside?" asked Angelo.

"Do you have a warrant?"

"Right here." Angelo widened his jacket so Dante could see the firearm inside. "Fresh from the judge."

It was another old line, an old routine. Someone didn't want to talk, a glimpse of the firearm sometimes loosened them up. Judge, trial, and jury. Angelo gave him his brotherly smile. When they had worked together, back when, Angelo had been the one with the soft soap. The hard end of the stick, that had been Dante's end of things.

"You chief yet?" Dante said, another one of their old lines, funny once, but not so funny anymore. These conversations, even then, they'd had a tendency to go the wrong way.

"I have my opportunities."

"It's nice, you have such a good attitude."

Angelo spoke softly. "You're a bitter fuck."

"Better than no fuck at all."

"I wouldn't know. I've never had that problem."

"No?"

"I'm happily married."

"So I've heard."

It wasn't a kind thing to say. Angelo had been to the brink of a divorce. Maybe it was the autistic kid at home. Or the usual midlife stuff. Or the fact that his career, while good enough, was not exactly where he'd wanted it to be.

"Let me see the paperwork."

"It's coming," said Angelo. "The boys are on their way from the courthouse."

"It's true," Chin repeated. "The warrant's on its way."

It was possible they were bluffing. He'd done so himself, back in the day, just to get inside, to take a look around before the suspect cleaned the place out.

"All right."

He made the slightest gesture, as if moving toward the door, but the thick-neck put a hand on his shoulder.

"I think we'll be a little more comfortable," said Angelo, "if you let Sergeant Jones here check your person."

"I have a firearm, under the shoulder. It's licensed."

"I'm sure it is," said Angelo. "Now, if you empty out your pockets, my friend here, he'd like to give you a little bit of a thrill."

Dante dumped his cell and his keys and all his change.

"Open your jacket."

Dante did as he was told. The big blond reached in and took the gun from its holster, then patted him down. He wasn't too gentle about it. Big hands under the shoulders. Knifing up between the legs.

"Do it again," said Angelo.

"What?" asked the sergeant.

"Between the legs."

Sergeant Jones did as he was told, knifing up a second time. "There's nothing."

"As I suspected," said Angelo.

TWELVE

It was difficult to tell Chin's age by looking, but there was an iron streak in her hair, and in this light, if only for a moment, he could see the hard lines on her face. She had not changed much since the last time Dante had seen her, though she allowed herself small adornments these days: simple earrings and a faint gloss on her lips. Meanwhile, Angelo strolled about his apartment, peering into everything. Rule was, situation like this—when a civilian invited you into their place—you could look but not touch. Not unless something jumped out at you.

"Bit of a mess here."

"I haven't had a chance to clean."

"Looks like someone's been rummaging."

"Corkscrew," Dante said. "I had a bottle of wine I wanted to open."

"What vintage?"

"Red."

"You keep it in the cellar?" Angelo nodded toward the basement door.

"You'll have to wait for the warrant."

Angelo tilted his head, cocking his ears—a gesture almost comic, doglike.

"Did you hear that?"

"No."

"I should take a look. I'm concerned there might be someone else on the premises."

"I don't think so."

"That noise—in the basement? Do you hear it, Lieutenant Chin?"

This, too, was part of the routine. There had been no noise, and they all three knew it. Angelo waited for the nod from Chin. It was a common-enough tactic: a pretense for poking around without a warrant—but Chin still did not respond, not wanting to do anything that would jeopardize the case or spoil the evidence in the eyes of a judge, in the event they found whatever it was they were after.

Ultimately, it did not matter.

Because suddenly there was a car outside. The alley was narrow and the car pulled up on the walk, and another car pulled up close behind.

The warrant boys had arrived.

Chin sat across from him, in the sagging chair that had been his father's. She was somewhere in her fifties, though it took more than a single glance to make the calculation. Maybe it was on account of the Chinese skin, or because of the San Francisco fog, shielding the sun, but her face did not hold its age. Rather the age lines came and went, according to the light, and in this particular light, they had vanished altogether. She had grown up around the corner, back when the Italians still outnumbered the Chinese, and the dago toughs still ruled the corners down on Stockton. She had her own reasons for pursuing the Wus. Years ago, one of her relatives had been shot to death in the Imperial Restaurant.

"You'll find my financials in a plastic box upstairs," said Dante, "but you're not going to find it interesting. Nothing from the warehouse. I don't have much to do with that."

"I'm aware of your financials," said Chin.

Something flickered across her face, and he realized this search, it was about something else. Angelo was with homicide, after all. He felt dread rise in his stomach.

"You've already got my Glock," he said. "There's a Wesson upstairs, a .45. Registered—in a holster, in my closet."

"I'll tell them," she said.

He did not mention the stiletto, blade concealed, spring-loaded in its metal case that resembled an old-fashioned cigarette lighter. If they found it, he'd say it had been his father's, a keepsake—though this wasn't true. Meanwhile, he could hear the warrant boys in the garage. Often as not, the cops took the owners off premises during a search like this, unless they thought you might help them in some way, or if they wanted to study your reaction as they searched.

"If you tell me what you're looking for, maybe we can cut this short."

"Where were you when this place was ransacked?"

Dante had already described the evening for Chin, how Marilyn had been here for a little while, and how after that he'd gone to the Naked Moon. He did not tell her about the prostitute, though, or the business at the Sam Wong.

"You didn't call the police?"

"About the break-in? No."

"Why not?"

"I know how busy you all are."

"It seems to me, whoever came through here, it appears they were looking for something."

"Kids," Dante said. "They made a mess. They took a crap in the toilet. Broke a vase."

"What did they take?"

"I don't know. I haven't had a chance to go through it all. But there wasn't anything of value here."

"It seems like they might have taken the Wesson. Or your mother's jewelry."

"I guess they didn't find it."

If Chin was skeptical, her face did not show it. It did not show much at all. Her lip gloss was pale, and there was the slightest shadow on her eyes.

"I've been talking to your cousin, you know that."

"Yes."

"I advised him to turn state's evidence."

"I don't think he was crazy about the idea."

"We were supposed to meet, but he didn't show up."

Chin gave him a gray-eyed look, empty, revealing nothing—
but that emptiness itself, it told him everything. "The last
time you saw him, when was that?"

"We've been through this."

"Tell me again."

It was a mixed crew searching the house—Angelo's
people and Chin's, homicide and SI—and there was only
one reason homicide would be along. Dante hoped he was
mistaken. Chin got up all of a sudden, leaving him in the
room with Sergeant Jones, the hulking cop with the blond
crew cut and the thick neck and the fat jaw. Interrogators
liked to do this sometimes, just leave you sitting while they
thought it over, piecing it together in their heads. He heard
a thumping in the attic. The warrant boys rummaged above
him now, handing boxes down to Angelo in the kitchen,
yukking it up as they worked. He caught a glimpse of Chin
through the window, out in the street, talking into her cell.

Dante waited with the thick-necked cop in his father's
den. The cop was admiring the old RCA, a tube model
with the rabbit ears on top.

"This thing work?"

"Sure."

The cop bent down. "Which knob?"

"The one in the center."

"This one?"

"Push."

"Nothing happens."

"You have to plug it in."

The man bent over, reaching for the plug. Dante felt the

urge to leap up and knock the son of a bitch over the head, for all the good it would do.

"It's plugged in now."

"Takes a while to warm up."

"How long?"

"Not long."

"It doesn't work, does it? You're pulling my leg."

"You're a bright guy."

"You think you're funny."

"It just takes a little while to warm up. It's got tubes. Put your hand on top of the cabinet. You'll feel the heat."

"I don't feel anything."

Dante remembered his grandfather, the fisherman, watching the old shows. *Queen for a Day. Supermarket Sweep. The Milton Berle Show,* with Milton himself, the big Jew, dressed in drag, strutting across the stage. The old man watched with the El Producto hanging from his lips, laughing his head off—blowing smoke through that enormous nose. Of course, the television didn't work anymore and hadn't worked for years. The set had been a problem even in its prime: the tuner came off in your hand, so you had to turn the channels with a pair of pliers, then jiggle the antennae forever until the snow and the static disappeared. Now the cop stood with his hand on the cabinet, waiting for that light at the center of the picture tube to spring large and fill the screen. But it wasn't going to happen. All the light and sound had collapsed into a tiny square years ago, a pinprick, vanished into darkness, and it was never going to spring back.

The cop took away his hand. "It doesn't work," he said.

"You have to be patient."

"You're a real card. A regular joker."

"No. You're the card."

Angelo appeared in the doorway holding a carton his buddies had dragged from the attic.

"What's going on in here?"

"Sergeant Jones is interested in my father's television."

Dante recognized the box Angelo held, a carton full of his mother's baubles, things she'd had in the asylum, hairbrush, Polaroids, news clippings, bundles of unmailed letters she'd written in her final years, notes to Pope John XXIII, Holy Father in Rome. To Al Capone and Marie Antoinette. Letters intermingling world events with family business, confessing guilt one moment, innocence the next, a complex tissue of associations in which it was impossible to separate the real from the imagined.

"Put that down," said Dante.

Once upon a time, he and Frank Angelo had been friends, more or less. Working the beat together, they both had known the way it was in the neighborhood, or the way it had been. Backdoor whorehouses that the cop station left alone. Highstakes card games at Portofino's. Underage kids dry-humping Fiora Pistola on the dance floor while her husband triplecharged them for drinks. There was a lot of little stuff that as a cop you didn't do anything about, and a lot of big stuff, too, depending. All the rumors about the Mancuso warehouse back then, they'd reached a fever pitch, it seemed, when he had been Angelo's partner. Angelo who'd been like a brother to him, both of them up for promotion at the same time.

"What are you looking for?"

One of the warrant boys brought in another box and put it at Angelo's feet. The box had his mother's name on it, written in big letters in his father's hand, and Dante remembered the day his father had packed it, not so long after she died, going through her clothes, hand-folding her blouses, her skirts, and laying these articles one at a time into the box. Angelo put his hand into the carton: his partner, soft-hearted Angelo, taunting him in a way Dante had seen him do before, just like this, on the job, trying to get a suspect to blow. "I remember the day the doctors picked her up. I remember her out on the sidewalk there, screaming and hollering." Angelo took one of the dresses in his stubby hands. Behind Angelo, Dante saw Chin returning.

"This was what she was wearing, wasn't it?"

Dante stood up then. He'd had enough. He meant to take the dress away from Angelo, put it back in the box, but Dante moved too quickly, too rash, and the big cop wasn't taking any chances. Or Jones was still mad about the television. Either way, the big cop got him from behind with a slapjack to the head.

Dante went down.

He lolled painfully on the carpet, peering up through the cracked light. Angelo peered back down, and Chin did, too. The hard lines were back in her face, but whether that hardness was for him or for Angelo, he didn't know. Maybe she had some reservations about the way Angelo had provoked him, or maybe she didn't see it that way. Cops crossed the line all the time. Out of necessity, or because it was a frustrating job, the crooks were assholes, and you had to get your pleasure where you could.

Dante understood this. Or had understood once. It was harder to understand rolling on the floor, wincing into that cracked light.

She and Angelo were talking.

"CSI?"

"They sent it over."

"The photograph, yes."

"Show it to him," said Angelo.

"Give him a minute."

Dante did not want to see. He had already guessed what they were about to show him, and he did not want to see. In the old days, it took time to get the photos developed. These days, the CSI cars had a printer embedded in the dash, hooked up to the wireless, and out it came. There weren't enough cops on the street, the hydrants didn't work, but the city had plenty of money for this kind of stuff. Dante lay there, holding his head. The big cop got down on his hands and knees and propped the photo against the couch leg. It was a crummy print, with the color all lousy, and in the middle of that lousy color, Gary Mancuso lay twisted and dead.

"Déjà vu," said Angelo.

THIRTEEN

The way the neck hung, the slash in the esophagus, the narrow band that encircled the throat—Dante had seen it before. His cousin had been strangled with a steel sling, a simple device: a length of wire affixed at each end to a wooden dowel. It wasn't hard to kill somebody this way, but it took some practice, some training. Approach the victim from behind, loop the cord over the head.

Dante had seen similar photos when he was with the company, traveling abroad. A diplomat's son had been murdered in this manner, then his wife, strangled a week apart. Eventually, the diplomat had been arrested, and had hanged himself in jail.

Murder-suicide, the police had concluded, though Dante knew better. The deceased diplomat had been peddling information, working both sides. And there'd been similar cases in Toronto, in Bonn.

The company did not tolerate betrayal.

A simple move, one motion. Turn around, pivot, back to back with the victim, still holding the dowels, yanking. Then bend at the waist. Not a deep bend, but far enough so that the victim's feet came off the ground, so the killer and the victim were one self, one beast, a two-headed animal, if only for a moment, joined at the spine, with two feet on the ground and the other two in the air, arms flailing up top.

The secret was in the first move, after looping the wire over the head. When the killer turned, the wire crossed, cinching the victim's neck. After that, it was easy. Just bend, hold tight. Let gravity do the rest.

D ante had been in the gray room before. If not this exact room, then rooms like it. He had sat on every side of the table, in every chair. He'd been the kiss-ass cop who brought the coffee and the Snickers bar, sweet-talking the witness, and he'd been the bulldog in a spiked collar lunging at the throat. He'd been the invisible snoop, the man on the other side of the one-way glass, plotting the interrogation.

He'd also been in the position he now occupied. A person of interest, as the phrase went. A suspect in the matter at hand.

Angelo and Chin had driven him from his father's place to the station downtown. They had talked to him together for a little while. Now it was just Chin.

She pulled the blind on the observation window and killed the mike and the audio recorder, too. None of that meant anything necessarily, because she could have a wire up her sleeve, for all he knew, or there could be a tiny video camera in the lamp. Or she could just write it all down in her notepad after she walked out of here, truth or lie, it didn't matter. In the end, nothing, anywhere, was confidential.

"After you left the force, you lived in New Orleans."

"Seven years."

"Private security?"

"Export firm."

"Sometimes you went abroad?"

"They did imports, too. Intracompany stuff, mostly. Sometimes, you know, between here and there, there would be a shortfall."

"And you'd have to track it down."

"Or not."

"But the pay was good?"

"Good enough."

"Why did you come back?"

"I was raised here."

Her face gave him nothing. Chin was in Special Investigations, so she had access to things and could make her own deductions. Perhaps she'd penetrated to his other life, the one in which he'd been deep cover, officially unaffiliated, in an organization within an organization, down in that murky area, the shadowland. In the government flowchart, SI had connections to Homeland, and Homeland connected to the CIA and the NSA, with lines going back and forth, and then outside all that, off the chart, nameless, unlabeled, were the boxes connected by invisible lines.

Chinn was savvy enough to suspect that his job had been out there, in the space outside the lines.

"Given your ownership interests in the warehouse, you will need to talk to the Wus. There are business concerns to untangle."

"What do you want?"

"The investigation doesn't stop. Your name—it's on the deed."

"I can't help you."

"You have to talk to the Wus, one way or the other. They'll make you an offer of some sort, even if it's just to buy you off, send you away. I want you to tell me what they offer."

"And if I don't?"

She shrugged off the question. "We can offer you protection," she said. "You won't have to answer to the Wus."

He didn't believe her any more than his cousin had believed her. She couldn't protect him.

"I'll think about your offer," he said, though in truth he had no intention. If he talked to the Wus, it would be for his own reasons.

Chin was pretty good at holding her face empty, but it slipped, and he saw her weariness. Her face, her eyes, they showed her age, but at the same time, he could see the schoolgirl with the pleated dress and the skinny legs and the piercing expression. She'd gone to the Salesian School, run by the Saints Peter and Paul Church, same as he had gone. They shared that much, anyway.

"You're making a mistake," said Chin.

She left him alone in the gray room. He expected to be sitting at the table for some time, staring at those dull walls. He expected the sweet stuff was over and sooner or later, she and Angelo would be back, working in tandem or pairs, bringing in a third buddy, then a fourth, not letting him sleep, trying to wear him down. They could charge him in the murder, or just take him down to the holding tank and let him sit there overnight. He thought about his cousin. About Marilyn, unprotected. He had made a mistake, no doubt, though it wasn't the mistake Chin thought. She and Angelo meant to hold him, he determined, the only question was for how long. As it turned out, he was wrong about that as well. The next person to appear was neither Angelo nor Chin, but the sergeant who minded the hall.

"You're free to go."

FOURTEEN

Ten years ago, Dante had driven across the Mississippi River to a small office in Algiers across from New Orleans. He had walked up some long steps and talked to a man in that office and the man had sent him across the way, to a phone booth on the Rue Sangre. The booth was hot and the connection was poor. The voice inside the static gave him an assignment, a place to go, an agent to meet. In the years since, Dante had never gotten used to the sound of the voice. He was often tempted to go back to Algiers, walking up the stairs to the office where the small man had hunched over the desk, but he knew it would not be the same and the man would be long gone. As it was, Dante could not shake the feeling that he had never left, that once he'd crossed the river to that other side, there was no going back—no matter what self-deception he practiced, he was forever in that phone booth with his ear pressed to the receiver, listening to the insect on the other side.

Now he lingered in the shadows outside Marilyn's house, insubstantial, a shadow himself, watching, to be sure she was safe. That was all he wanted. The cops had confiscated his guns, but they'd not found the stiletto, and he carried it now in his pocket. A woman passed by, harmless. Then a couple, arm in arm, headed up the hill. Before he'd left the force, when his father was still alive, there'd been a moment, like the moment with Chin, when he could have cooperated with the investigation, but he hadn't done so. He could have cooperated, to hell with his family, and had some kind of other life, here with Marilyn. Instead, he'd left her and gone to New Orleans.

Someways, things had come full circle. Except now it was more complicated, more dangerous. Dominick Greene was still staying in the Wong, and spent his afternoons in the cafés and his evenings wandering the clubs along Broadway, and ended up often as not in the Melody Lounge. Dante knew this much about Greene already, and he would know more soon, he hoped, because he'd put in a call to Jake, down at Cicero Investigations, asking his boss to run a make. Meanwhile, a car pulled up, a Mercedes. Then in a little while, Marilyn came down with David Lake. Dressed for the opera.

Lake was a good man.

Dante knew this because he'd looked into Lake's past as well, playing it nosy, back when the man had first appeared in Marilyn's life. The fact of Lake's goodness, though, didn't make it any easier, watching the two of them climb into the car. The Mercedes drove down the hill, its taillights flaring in the twilight.

Then Dante went to the Naked Moon.

He still needed to talk to Rossi, but the man wouldn't be home, not yet, and in the meantime he still hoped to find the girl. But the dancer was not there, and she was not at her room down in the flats. Her disappearance was coincidence, he told himself again. Meanwhile, there were places girls like her ended up. He caught a taxi then down to South of Market, to a spot under the freeway, where the hard-core girls worked the corner, hailing passersby, and in between clients, the girls got on their knees, crawling through a break in the fence, to a concrete field where you could buy just about any drug you wanted.

"Slow down," he said.

The driver obliged.

The girl was not among those on the corner. He peered through the taxi window toward the darkness underneath the freeway. Maybe the girl was there, with the users, and he was tempted for a minute to follow her into those shadows. Because he wanted to know if Greene had sent her, he told himself, though maybe that was not the reason at all. Because it was time for him to disappear, too. He'd seen Marilyn on Lake's arm. He closed his eyes, full of yearning, and his nostrils widened, as if taking in the acrid smoke from the foil, and he remembered the girl touching him, back in the elevator.

"What next?" asked the driver.

Dante reached into his pocket, touched the stilletto in its case. If I disappear, he thought, if I vanish from the face of the earth, Marilyn becomes irrelevant. They won't be able to move against me by hurting her, but he wasn't sure how to accomplish that, not yet. Or maybe he still hoped there was another way.

"Back the way we came," Dante said, and gave the man Rossi's address up on Russian Hill.

PART FOUR

FIFTEEN

In the end, it was the Sicilians. Not the Italians from Lucca, with their shops and their restaurants. Not the Calabrians, the peasants from the south. Not the Italian Swiss, the industrious ones, with their chocolate factories and canneries and their bank on the corner of Columbus. These others might have the good life, some of them, but it was not them, in the end, who owned the Beach. Rather it was the old Sicilians in their torn sweaters.

Old men lounging on the green benches in Washington Square.

A million dollars in torn sweaters.

Fish money.

The former mayor, Joe Rossi, was of this line. He lived in a yellow house at the top of Russian Hill—a gambrel-roofed Victorian with a private yard in the back. It was crab money, fisherman money, a share of the wharf, purchased by Rossi's own father years ago. The Sicilians had outfished the Luccans and outbullied the Chinese, controlled the bay until the shrimp beds were dry and the sardines fished out, and then they'd made other arrangements. But it was all fish money when you got down to it. Dredged out of the sea and wrestled onto the wharf. It was fish money that had financed Joe Rossi's career, and fish money now that was financing his daughter's run. Fish money once removed, but it still had the same smell. You didn't get rich, unless you were willing to stink, Dante's father used to say, and you didn't stay rich if you dressed in anything other than a torn sweater.

Mayor Rossi had dispensed with the torn sweater part of this wisdom. He showed his money and thought himself a good man, though there were plenty of people who would tell you otherwise. Some of the enmity was personal, and some of it was for convenience' sake—because everyone had to hate someone—and some of it was over political business from long ago.

Good man or no, he would do anything for his daughter. Gennae Rossi was the light of her father's eye. She'd been a teenager when her father was mayor, and her picture had been in the society page when she married. She'd worked in the welfare kitchens after college and given her fish money to the poor. Barely thirty when she was elected to the city council, elegant and modest both at once, so poised, posture like a saint until the multiple sclerosis.

Rossi himself did not answer the door. Rather it was his wife, dressed in such a way—in a formal dress, sashed at the waist—that suggested they had just returned from the evening's event. She'd had a mastectomy six months ago, and though you could not tell by looking, rumor among the old ones, down at Serafina's, claimed the long-range prognosis was not good, and old Mayor Rossi, these days, was sleeping in the study. Whether this was on account of his own trouble getting up the stairs or repulsion at his wife's cancer—this depended upon whom you talked to, but either way the couple was active in their daughter's campaign.

Given the hour, and the fact of his cousin's outburst, Dante half expected Mrs. Rossi might send him away. Her husband, though, had spent a long time in public life. She had seen people come and go, at all hours, and if she held his cousin's behavior against him, she did not show it. Mrs. Rossi was, at any rate, affable by nature.

"We just got back. Gennae was speaking this evening, at Il Cenacolo." She smiled. "Joe introduced her." Il Cenacolo was an Italian group that met once a month, businessmen mostly, political types, people with money. Gennae's candidacy was a long shot, and her father was not loved by everyone, but they'd turned out like in the old days, elbow to elbow around the white table cloths, raising their glasses. "It was nice," she said.

"How's the campaign?"

"There's a surge."

"Oh."

"That's what Joe says. He can feel these things."

"I imagine he can."

His words came out wrong, too sardonic, and Mrs. Rossi became haughty then. She held her head in profile, nose turned—but he felt no enmity toward her. She was one of the few who'd gone down to visit his mother after she'd been placed in the asylum.

"It's good to see you," she said. Mrs. Rossi turned on her heel, as if to head up the long stairs behind her.

"Just go in."

"Excuse me."

"The study. He's resting in there. Only an idiot would climb these stairs."

M ayor Rossi lounged in his study, leaning back in his big chair, feet on the ottoman, shoes off. He lay with the chair tilted all the way back, hands folded on his paunch, eyes closed, shirt open at the collar. His pajamas and a night robe lay draped nearby, and there was a pillow on the sofa, suggesting that might be his later destination. He had not made it there yet, though, into his pajamas and onto the sofa, but instead had wheezed off in his chair. If Rossi had heard Dante come in, he gave no immediate sign.

The room had that old wop smell.

Tobacco. Wine. Fish.

"Mayor?"

Rossi opened his eyes, taking stock of the younger man, and Dante was aware of the gulf between them. The mayor had been friends with his father, back in the day. He did not look quite awake.

"Don't you knock when you come in?"

"I did knock."

"That's what they all say." Rossi rubbed his eyes with his fists. "What brings you, this hour?"

"Business."

The old man grimaced up at him and struggled on the recliner, forcing the chair upright. "Your asshole cousin was here."

"Is that so?"

"Yes."

"My asshole cousin is dead."

The mayor didn't know how to take this. He laughed, or started to, a guffaw really, an odd chortle, cut short in the throat. Then he coughed. There was an ugly rattle in his chest. "You're not joking?"

"No."

The mayor leaned forward. The far wall, the other side of the room, chronicled Rossi's career—starting some sixty years back, just after World War II, black-and-white photos of a thick-chested man smiling into the camera, gung ho for the world. Closer by, on the desk itself, were pictures of the old man and his wife, at some lake in Italy, on their second honeymoon, wandering down the medieval streets. It was the kind of street on which Marilyn imagined herself, wearing a gown like the one Gennae Rossi wore in the wedding picture out in the hall.

"I'm sorry," said Rossi. "I had no idea."

"He came to see you?"

"The other day. We . . ." He shook his head. "What happened?"

Dante told him about the murder, and as he did so, he

studied Rossi's face. He studied it the same way Chin had studied his own, looking for what lay beneath the surface. There was always something hidden, but whether it mattered, whether it meant anything, that was harder to tell.

"What do the police think?"

"Gary was up here to see you, wasn't he?"

"Did you tell the police that?"

"What did he want?"

Rossi told him then, pretty much the same story Dante had gathered from Gary. Different in some particulars, but not the important ones. From the sound of it, his cousin had come up here, grabbing at straws, hoping the former mayor could somehow use his influence to squelch the investigation. "As if a word from me, his problems would go away. I wish people would listen to me like that." Rossi laughed dryly. "When I told him no, well . . . You know how he could be sometimes."

"Ugly."

"Yes."

"The police have already talked to me," said Dante. "Sooner or later, I guess, they will talk to you as well. But there's no reason for the media to come along."

"What are you saying?"

"I know how much you love your daughter."

"Don't play that card on me."

"A story like this—a time like this—the candidate's father, the ex-mayor, questions concerning the murder of a man seeking a favor in regard to a criminal investigation . . ."

Mayor Rossi had suffered a million accusations in the past,

charges of corruption, of playing his connections for financial benefit, and though some of them were true, at least in part, he'd walked the line and fended them all off. He glared at Dante with the old wop defiance, but at the same time his countenance was creased with exhaustion. He had pulmonary problems and his wife was dying of cancer, but none of that was what bothered him. He didn't want the campaign coming apart on their daughter.

"What, then, do you want?"

"Ru Shen's diary . . ."

The mayor shook his head. "What does that have to do with your cousin?"

"Someone's been leaking information."

"Your cousin?"

"You tell me."

During a trip to China, Ru Shen had disappeared. This was common knowledge. It was not widely known, however, that his body had been found in the cargo hold of a container ship, by the immigration authority. It had gone unidentified at first, and Ru Shen's effects—including the journal—had been bagged and stored, then subsequently destroyed. The mayor's fear of the journal back then, three years ago, had had little to do with the company. Rossi's concerns were more prosaic. He had been involved in a number of questionable deals over the years, but what worried him most was what had happened on a particular junket. Small stuff, ultimately, regarding a couple of girls in a Hong Kong hotel room.

"No," Rossi said. "Your cousin said nothing about the journal."

There was a tremor in the old man's voice. Near the picture on the desk, of himself and his wife in Italy, there stood a photo, Gennae, in her bright blouse, gold earrings. She smiled a big smile. Her father's smile.

"She did good tonight," said the old man. "She can move a crowd."

"I've seen."

"She has a light about her."

"The diary," Dante interrupted. "Is there another copy?"

Joe Rossi put his head into his hand. "I'm sorry. It's just, this campaign is important to Gennae. And she doesn't need some nonsense in the paper. I don't need this."

"No one cares about fifteen minutes you spent with a girl in a hotel room twenty years ago."

"Then what?"

"Is there a copy?"

Rossi walked over to his wall, the one with all the photos of the old days, showing how he'd started as a young lawyer, out there in front of the crab house, smelling of fish, standing in the midst of the men with the torn sweaters. From there he'd worked himself up to judge, then mayor, surrounded by every businessman in town. His daughter, in her wheelchair, was trying to follow the same path behind him. From Rossi's posture, the way he stood now, Dante understood that the old man knew she wasn't going to make it. She was too far behind. Even so, he did not want some tawdriness spoiling her campaign.

"The Chinese Historical Society, maybe."

"What?"

"It's possible," Rossi said.

The mayor explained how, before Ru Shen's body was identified, the Chinese Historical Society had been involved in a special project, gathering the effects of stowaways. It was possible, Rossi supposed, they'd rummaged Ru Shen's effects as well, not knowing who he was, not caring, simply gathering artifacts of stowaways to be stored as part of their collection. Immigration had allowed them to make facsimiles of such documents, but so far as Rossi knew, whatever they'd found sat in a box, in the basement of the Historical Society.

"You never checked."

"It seemed best, you know, to leave well enough alone. And like you said, who cares now, what an old man did in a hotel room."

"It was never cataloged?"

"The grant ran out." The mayor shrugged. "Then recently, they got some money. For 'Across the Water'—that exhibit."

It was the kind of thing that happened in the city. Projects were initiated, papers gathered, then left to gather dust. Then, sooner or later, someone came along and stirred it all up. Dante had seen the workers, just the other day, dismantling the last phase of "Across the Water" down at Portsmouth Square.

"The Wus financed that?"

"In part. There was a fuss in the paper."

That, too, was the kind of squabbling that happened after those sorts of things, mutually funded, in which the parties disagreed as to where the items should be permanently housed. In this case, some of the artifacts had disappeared, and there were allegations back and forth.

"My wife . . ."

The old man's eyes went soft, and Dante saw Rossi's concern, worried that all of a sudden, his old indiscretions would become public.

"Don't worry," Dante said.

Rossi nodded his head, not quite convinced. Once, he could have interfered, but Rossi didn't have the resources or stamina anymore.

Dante put his hand on the old man's shoulder. "Go to sleep," he said.

Dante left. The fuss regarding "Across the Water" had died down as quickly as it started, he remembered, the allegations withdrawn. Even so, the insinuation had been clear enough at the time. The artifacts had been taken by the Benevolent Association itself, for its private collection, carried across the square, up into the chambers of Love Wu.

SIXTEEN

He woke up later, alone in his bed with the image of Marilyn in that velvet dress, in her black wrap, crossing the road, Lake beside her, heading to the opera house at dusk. He lay sleepless, thinking of her and of his dead cousin, and of Dominick Greene, in residence at the Sam Wong.

He and Marilyn were supposed to meet later today, midmorning, down at the marina, at the slip where he docked his grandfather's boat. Only Marilyn called, just past nine.

"I'm going to be late," she said.

"Oh."

"My couple."

"What about them?"

"They called me up just a few minutes ago. There's a place they want to see."

For the past week or so, Marilyn had been showing a couple around North Beach, some newcomers with money, looking for a place to buy but staying meantime in the Stanford Court, halfway up Nob Hill. They had cash, they claimed, having just sold their place in Barcelona. Meantime, today, just before lunch, there was a two-bedroom they wanted to see, over in Noe Valley, on the other side of the city, so Marilyn wouldn't be able to meet him till almost one.

"All right?"

"Of course."

There was something in her voice, subdued, and something in his own voice, too, when he responded. Things between him and Marilyn, they had reached a tipping point, and maybe that was a good thing, given the circumstances. He needed to cut her loose. For her own safety, if nothing else. He worried, though, that he had waited too long.

"I'll see you at one," he said.

Jake Cicero had been running his investigative business for almost thirty years, out of a third-story office in a brick building that stood on a terrace over the Broadway Tunnel. Dante had been working for Cicero for some time, and he knew the man's habits well. The front office looked out into the neighborhood, and that was where Jake sat when he talked on the phone, at that window, his Italian loafers up on the metal desk.

"Someone has been making us," said Cicero. "Either that, or we got a fish."

"What makes you say that?"

"A gray sedan, out front."

"Now?"

"Yesterday. Twice."

Dante had called to check the book on Dominick Greene, but Cicero was more concerned with the come-and-go outside the building. It was a hobby of Cicero's, trying to figure the business of passersby, and he indulged that hobby when his own business was slow. There was the apartment building across the way, and an accounting firm on the floor above, and a marijuana dealer around the corner, and over the years, he'd gotten pretty good at guessing who was going where. Private investigation wasn't exactly a walk-in business, but there were still those who lingered on occasion outside. Disgruntled crooks. Spouses, pissed they'd been caught in the act. Plainclothes cops looking to nab one of Cicero's criminal clients in violation of parole.

"Did you get a look?"

"Guy never got out of the car. But there was a woman out there as well. Same vehicle, later in the day."

"You sure."

"The woman got out. Walked up to the building. Then back out. Checking the directory."

"Wrong building, maybe."

"Divorce case. She had that look."

"Except she didn't come up."

"Embarrassed, you know how they are. Not sure she wants to hire someone, not yet. But she'll be back."

"You should know."

Cicero laughed. He had been divorced three times himself, and spent a good deal of his career tracking unfaithful husbands. It was still a good part of the firm's business, though these days they made their bread and butter on contract work from the public defender's office, looking for mitigating circumstances for career criminals.

"What about Greene?"

"Nothing much."

"No?"

"Why are you so interested?"

"Just tell me what you have."

Cicero went over it. Greene's father was a businessman, Garment District, New York City. Greene himself had done a stint in the army. Worked now for a fabric importer. Unmarried, traveled a lot. No criminal record. Nothing to make it seem like he was anything other than he claimed: a business rep looking for the cheapest way to get his goods to market. On the surface of it, anyway, the man's file sounded much like Dante's own, back when he'd worked in New Orleans.

"This guy—he have something to do with Gary?" asked Cicero.

"I don't know."

"You're not telling me."

"Later, we'll talk."

Dante did not want to get Cicero further involved if he could help it. Meanwhile, If Ru Shen's journal had been in "Across the Water," as the mayor suspected, it would be on the manifest, over at the Chinese Historical Society. Dante didn't need to meet Marilyn until one, so he headed down there. As it turned out, the place kept odd hours, and the room he needed to visit, Special Collections, was closed on Fridays. So he found himself aimless in Chinatown. There was the softest breeze, no fog, a nice day for going out on the water, as good as it gets, but at the same time, he could feel the day heating, the air thickening with the smell of the Chinese stalls, the dried fish, the twisted duck, the bok choy, all mixed with the smell of the asphalt and the crowds, people close together, perspiring in cheap nylon. Above it all, hovered the Empress Building.

SEVENTEEN

The Empress was not an easy building to navigate. Over the years, its seven stories had been carved up in incomprehensible ways, so that halls ended suddenly and the office numbering was askew. The lower corridors smelled of cheap veneer and cleaning fluid, and a sign at the end of one of these corridors listed the second story businesses: money exchange and employment services, travel and real estate, legal assistance for immigrants. These offices could be attained by stair or by elevator but Dante was not interested. The offices of the Wu family themselves, and their intimates—those were higher up and harder to reach.

Both the stairwell and the elevator went only as far as the third floor. To get higher access, he had to negotiate the receptionist in the third-floor lobby, then the security office at the end of another hall.

"I'd like to see Love Wu."

The receptionist regarded him blankly. It was the face he always got in Chinatown, though he had seen the woman's cheek tremble. Fear—the suspicion she was being mocked. No one asked to see Love Wu, not if you were from the neighborhood and knew the stories. It was an arrogant thing to do.

"What is your name?"

"Mancuso."

Dante did not know his cousin's contact here. He was relying on the arrogance of his request—together with the card he slid across the desk, bearing the name of the family warehouse. The receptionist got on the phone, speaking Chinese, her voice rising, falling, and in that glottal music, the sudden pitch and yaw, he heard the sound of his own name. She uttered it again a little later, talking to someone a little higher in the building, he supposed, then again, and with each utterance his name seemed more foreign, less his own. The receptionist pointed him toward a plastic chair.

"You may wait," she said.

As he sat, a young nurse came up the stairs from the street, from the same direction he himself had come. She was Chinese, with dark eyes and darker hair. She had porcelain skin and delicate features, and she carried a shopping bag from one of the downtown stores. She skimmed over him with her sharp black eyes, a fleeting look, regarding him in much the same way the receptionist had, as if she were glancing through him, seeing him without seeing. Then she put her access card in the elevator slot and went up.

Eventually, two young men sauntered from the security office down the hall, big-shouldered boys who looked as if they took a special pleasure in bouncing people into the street. One was big-boned, with a face from the Mongolian plains, but the other was a small man, quick-eyed and nervous. They took him to the elevator. Once the door closed, the pair gave him the same treatment he'd gotten from Angelo and the thick-necked cop out on Fresno Street a couple days before. The Mongol lurked behind him while the smaller man patted Dante down, touching him in all the usual places.

"Why are you here?"

"I have business with Mr. Wu."

"Love Wu," the small one said, his voice dripping, and Dante guessed the boys from security were among those the receptionist had been talking to.

"Who do you think you are?"

Dante told him his name.

"That's not what I mean. I mean just who do you think you are?"

"He's not doing much thinking, you ask me."

"A business associate," said Dante.

"The Benevolent Association has lots of partners. They don't come without appointments."

"Apparently, there are exceptions. You've been told to bring me up."

"What year do you think this is? You think this is 1878?"

"He thinks we are little Chinamen with pigtails, this is what he thinks."

"You think it is the year of the monkey?"

"He thinks we wear red silk jackets and sell egg rolls on the street."

"He thinks maybe he can find himself a yellow mistress."

"Maybe he is an admirer of the Orient."

"He wants a yellow girl to scrub his toilets."

"Is that why you came here, looking for a yellow girl?"

"No," said Dante. "I don't want a yellow girl."

"What's the matter, not good enough for you?"

"You don't like the way we smell?"

"No. I love the way you smell," said Dante.

"What did you say?"

Dante held his tongue. The Mongol stiffened behind him, and the other one clenched his jaw. There wasn't much space in the elevator. Dante could sense the boys struggling, wanting to let loose, but what Dante had said was true: They'd been told to bring him up. Any trouble along the way, there'd be explaining to do, and that explaining wouldn't be worth the pleasure of knocking around this Italian with the big nose. They rode the rest of the way in silence.

The elevator went only as far as the sixth floor, one story short of the upper chambers. The two men guided him down the hall. On the way, they passed an open lift with an accordion door, and inside that lay a heap of dirty linen and a box of geriatric supplies. It was an old cargo lift, installed years ago, used to carry things up that final story. The men ushered him farther on, to an office with a waiting room. The door stood partially open, and he could hear voices beyond—a man and a woman.

A young woman stepped into view: the same woman he'd seen earlier in the lobby, the nurse, only now she wore a different blouse and stood in such a way, one hand on her waist, that suggested she was modeling her purchase.

"Very nice," the man said. His voice was appreciative— but the man himself remained unseen.

On the carpet, by the woman's heels, a shopping bag lay discarded. She walked over and pushed the door closed.

By the time it opened again and the boys from security led him through, the woman was gone. It was just a man behind a desk in shirtsleeves and glasses. Like Rossi, he had pictures of his wife and family at his elbow, and on the wall behind him hung certificates and honors of the type bestowed by the local chamber of commerce.

Yin was his name. Nelson Yin.

He wore a tie.

He had a Diet Coke on his desk.

Dante wondered where the young woman had gone. She had not left by the way Dante entered. It was an odd setup. The office had a second door, leading perhaps to an inner office, and he heard now on the other side of the wall the sound of footsteps, as of someone ascending a stair. In the corner behind Yin stood a statue of a goddess with a multitude of hands and four visages, so she faced in every direction all at once.

"I was looking to speak with Mr. Wu directly."

Yin smiled. "Which one? We are a big family."

"The one in the penthouse suite."

"There is no one in the penthouse suite."

Yin spoke in a matter-of-fact way, bemused, but Dante had seen the cargo lift and heard the nurse's footsteps and suspected there was something going on up there. From the looks of the scene he'd glimpsed through the office door—the way the young woman had stood, turning so as to show herself to Yin in her cheongsam—he suspected there was something else going on as well, which maybe the wife in the picture didn't know about.

"The elevator goes higher."

"Height does not always indicate ascendancy."

"You're in charge?"

"A family as large as ours—no one is in charge. We are an association."

"There is always someone in charge."

The fluorescent light played across Yin's glasses, obscuring his eyes—but in his voice there was a deeper bemusement. "Why are you here?"

"My cousin, he had business with you."

Yin did not respond. This silence, Dante read as assent. His cousin may not have dealt directly with Yin, but in the end, it did not matter. The business relationship, given its nature, would be masked in reams of paper.

"Do you know who killed my cousin?"

"How would I know such a thing?"

"You knew he was being investigated, I am sure. And if he were to cooperate in that investigation—"

"I know what you are implying. I would be offended, but I understand, you are speaking from grief. I am aware, too, that certain people in the police department have not given up a particular view of my family—but these investigations, they never go anywhere. And like I said, we are a large family."

"With no one in charge?"

Yin smiled again, a little too smugly, as if to let Dante know, yes, indeed, he was a man of power, but the nature of the smile itself undermined him, suggesting Yin did not have all the power he wanted.

On the wall behind him hung more family pictures. Yin with his family in front of a ranch home out in the suburbs. A house that was nice enough—but not ostentatious. A middle-management kind of house. Somewhere on the peninsula. Commuting distance. Other pictures showed Yin as a younger man, out in the Richmond District, posing with men of an earlier generation, and still others showed him here in China-town, standing in front of the Empress.

Dante glanced again at the many-headed goddess. At a row of texts in a glass bookcase. Chinese texts. Very old, some of them—collector's items. On top: a stack of magazines, some in Chinese, but not all. Fashion and travel, celebrity and de-sire. Property, perhaps, of the woman who'd disappeared up the stairs.

"You read Chinese?"

"To a small degree. After a couple generations, that gets lost."

"What about the girl?"

"The girl?"

"The nurse?"

Dante saw something in the man's face. Yin did not like the angle of discussion, perhaps, the prying into personal business, but it wasn't just that which Dante saw. It was the look of a man who was trapped. Not in the way Dante himself was trapped, but in a different way. A man trapped by the drive home, by the leather chair and the aging wife whom he lay with at night in an overlarge bed, in the moonlight falling through the sliding door. A man who had foolish dreams and knew they were foolish, but could not help but have them anyway. Those dreams had to do with the young nurse in the cheongsam blouse.

"Chin is determined to investigate," Dante said.

"Waterfront property, it always attracts rumors. There is such a thing as legitimate trade. From what I understand, your cousin was a good partner. If you are interested in continuing the association . . ."

"So you are making me an offer?"

"You came to me." Yin smiled more wanly now, thin-lipped, polite as could be, but the meaning was nonetheless clear. Keep a secret and we will prosper together. Whisper and everything comes undone.

"The police are going to put pressure on me—the same way they put it on my cousin."

"What do you want?" asked Yin.

According to the old stories, Love Wu's library was up-stairs, in his private chambers. The reason Dante had come here had little to do with his cousin. Rather, Dante had come here on reconnaissance, because if Ru Shen's journal was on the manifest, then he would need to make his way back, into that library, but he could not tell Yin that. His guess, Yin expected he had come for a piece of the business, in the wake of his cousin's death.

"I don't want anything," Dante said.

"Nothing?"

"I want nothing."

"Pardon?"

"What I am saying here—I have no intention of cooper-ating with the authorities, but I want no part of the business either."

"You want out."

"I don't want to end up like my cousin."

"I understand."

"So you can have it all. That's it. That's all I came to say."

Yin nodded, as if this were satisfactory. Dante did not know if the man believed him, but it didn't matter. He had given a reason for his appearance here. He had come to submit—to let them know he was not a threat. Likely, they did not believe him. Or could not afford the risk. Likely the world of the company and the Chinese underground overlapped—and Yin was already calculating a way to be rid of him. No matter, Dante's explanation had been good enough for now, and the brutes led him down back the way he had come. Dante walked out of the building, into

Portsmouth Square. He paused in front of the nameless hotel, where he studied the alley for a moment, the descending fire escapes. Then he kept going, away from the
Empress, thinking as he did about all those locked doors,
those labyrinthine passages, and the sound of the woman's
footsteps ascending behind the walls.

EIGHTEEN

His grandfather's felucca was docked in a slip down in the North Beach Marina. Dante had agreed to sell, some time before, to a young man who worked at the harbor. Dante hadn't wanted to let the boat go, but the marina had gone upscale. The slip fees were too much, the boat wasn't getting much use, and the yacht owners complained it was an eyesore. The young man who bought it planned to take it over to Sausalito, to have the engines overhauled, but he had told Dante he could take it out one last time.

Dante kept his eyes open at the boatyard. Examining the faces of the dockhands, of the wharf bums on the benches, the loungers with their beer bottles and foam cups. A man stood watching from the planking as he and Marilyn untethered the boat, then waved at the last moment, with the camaraderie of a fellow boater. Farther back, a woman leaned at the railing, chatting with her husband. There were others as well walking the pier—onlookers, bystanders, people with their own business, their own worries, killing time by the bay, though it was hard to know which passing glance, whose interest, was less casual than it seemed.

Marilyn had brought lunch in a basket. She stood in the prow of the ship in her sleeveless blouse and her sunglasses and her capris. The day was warm and she wore her hair tied back. The surface of the sea was bright and glassy, and something about how the light reflected brought out the scars on her face.

They headed out across the water, toward the island.

He studied a speedboat arcing across the water ahead, and studied, too, a sailboat that had left the dock behind them and some kayaks in close to shore, and other crafts, farther out, white sails like cocked hats, veering this way and that on the horizon.

Back on the shore, the bystanders grew small.

"This is nice," she said.

"Yes."

"It's idyllic."

"I think so."

"It clears my head just to be out here."

They were out in the middle of the channel, halfway to the island. He could see the refinery tanks squatting in the hills off to the east, and the bridge out to the west. When he and Marilyn were younger, he had taken her out toward the headlands and cut the engine and let it float. The current had taken them halfway to the Farallones, but they'd been too busy underdecks to notice.

She cut him a glance but did not say anything.

There was a cabin underneath—a small quarters with a fold-down bed and a gas burner and a dry closet for storage and portholes along the side for light. Marilyn went down there for a moment and came back up in some loose-fitting shorts. He could see now as well the scar tissue on the backs of her legs.

"It's hot."

"Yes."

The boat sputtered momentarily, and he felt the tug of the current, the slow pull out toward sea. Then the engine caught and they kept on going.

They docked on the other side of the island, downcurrent from the main beach. The island was uninhabited, except for the park service station—and the remains of the old military prison. Ferries ran back and forth to the island several times a day, carrying tourists and day hikers. The service made its last run at five, and it sometimes happened that a visitor missed the ferry and was stuck overnight, without gear, to sleep on the ground of the eucalyptus forest.

As they disembarked, Dante surveyed the sea behind him. No one had followed. There were a couple boats already in the cove, day travelers like themselves.

"Your blouse."

"Do you like it?"

"Sure."

Marilyn wore a sleeveless blouse that buttoned down the back—a bronze shade that brought out the color of her skin. She looked good, but the blouse wasn't one he had seen before, and it reminded him of David Lake and that trip to Santa Barbara. They walked past the old prison. It had been the holding ground for Chinese immigrants once upon a time, and the prisoners had scratched their names into the stone. Also the names of their beloved. Their towns of origin. Poems. Obscenities. The dark cubicles were filled with ideograms. A handful of Italians had been incarcerated there as well, at the start of World War II, for their allegiance to Mussolini, but they hadn't left any record behind.

From the steps, Dante could see over to San Francisco on one hand and back to Marin on the other—to those little towns scattered in the dappled light along the underside of those brown hills.

"I've got a new listing."

"Another one?"

"A nice place. An earthquake cottage."

"Marin?"

She nodded. After the earthquake, a hundred years ago now, refugees had thrown up shanties on the other side of the bay. Though most of those earthquake cottages were gone, the name was still used to describe bungalows built in the years since.

"Not too big. But there's lots of light."

"How much money?"

"It's affordable, relatively speaking. Some young couple will jump on it."

"I thought things were slow."

"It's a desirable property."

They hiked up along the ridge, and Marilyn took out her

basket and spread the blanket on the ground. He did not know how to broach what he had to say. He did not know if he wanted to. They talked about nothing. About the eucalyptus trees and how the park service was working to eliminate them in favor of native species, live oak and wild junca. About the color of the water down there in the shallows where the last boatload of tourists stood waiting to be hauled back.

"We're being left behind."

"Yes."

"We're on the island alone."

"It's not so bad."

"No."

"Do you want to see it?"

"What?"

"The place in Marin. I'm hosting an open house tomorrow afternoon."

"What about your clients? Those two you've been showing around."

"They'll be looking at it, too."

They walked down the rest of the way now, headed for the dock, bumping shoulders where the path narrowed. *I have to leave town.* The moment was slipping away. He had to end things some way or the other, because to do otherwise was to put her at risk. She would want an explanation, but he could not tell her why, because the knowledge itself would increase her danger. *Go with David Lake.* Though that alone, he knew, would not make her safe. Not so long as he himself were alive. Nor so long as they could get to him by going after her.

They headed across the gangway into the boat.

She went down into the hold, to put on warmer clothes, and he watched her dark form as she pulled the sweater over her head.

He stepped toward her. "My cousin," he said.

"Not now."

She pulled him into an embrace.

They lay in darkness belowdecks, but the darkness was not yet complete. He could see through the windows the hulking shape of the island, the dark lines of the eucalyptus, and also the white shimmering of the horizon, the edge of the sea and the sky, where the darker masses merged. There was the rocking of the boat, and the sound of the sea slapping against the hull, and the slow moan of the dock as it rolled and creaked with the evening breeze. The wind had picked up at dusk but then settled after the darkness fell. They talked about his cousin.

"What do the police think?"

"They're investigating. Gary was involved in some things."

"He was headed for a bad end."

"It looks that way."

"You talked to him?"

"A couple days before he died."

She looked uneasy, but he could not say he blamed her. Just weeks before, she had been down to Cabo with David Lake.

They stayed at a place along the coast there. A better choice, Lake.

Things might have been different, he told himself . . . if not for the company . . . if not for his cousin's foolishness . . . but this was not altogether true. . . . He'd had his chance to take her away. . . . They'd had their opportunities. . . .

Come with me.

He leaned over then and ran his fingers over her face. In the darkness of the hold, he could not see the scars, but they were still there. He could feel the mottling along her back and her thighs and her shoulders.

My fault.

Despite her flirtation with Lake, her growing attachment, she had kept coming to him. But this situation could not go on any longer.

Sometimes, in close quarters with her, he thought he could smell the other man's scent. He could smell the big house in Pacific Heights and the inside of the Mercedes and the polo shirts and the seat up in the opera box and the sweat in the guy's sand-colored hair. He could smell the other man as she moved toward him in the dark, under the white sheet—as she took his hand and put it down between her legs—as she wrapped herself around him and he buried his head into the hollow of her neck, and she herself started to sweat and labor, head tilted back, eyes toward the ceiling. Then he pulled her closer. Wanting just the smell of her body and her perfume and their clothes and those streets they had both known when they were kids. The scent of the two of them lying together in his father's house among all the boxes.

The boat rocked. The night rushed in. There was the quiet of the island behind them and the sound of the city in the distance.

"We could stay here tonight," she said.

"The space is tight."

"I don't want to go back."

"We have to."

Dante went above deck, looking toward the military prison. The Chinese immigrants there had been beaten and starved: by the Irish guards, the Germans, the Italians. But it was the tongs that had transported their kinsmen across the sea. Getting a fee from both sides—the laborers themselves and the employers who wanted them. It was the same business now, more or less.

Marilyn stood on the deck with the dark water behind her and the glittering city in the distance. She motioned toward the other shore. "It's over there."

"What?"

"The little house I was telling you about."

NINETEEN

Later, Dante would curse himself. He could have done things differently. He could have thought more clearly. He had known Greene was in the neighborhood, and he could have been more vigilant.

Instead, when they'd gotten back to the Beach that evening, he allowed himself to be carried away in the pleasure of walking beside her, down Grant, as he'd walked often enough before, lost in the scent of her so close to him, not wanting, not yet, to break the illusion. Marilyn had wanted to walk to a small grocery, a specialty place of sorts—high-end produce, imported chocolate and coffee, eggs from free-range chickens. It had seemed better to go with her than to let her go alone, but his attention had been on Marilyn herself, on her presence beside him, so he did not see Greene catty-corner across the way, nor did he see Greene enter the store behind them. He did not notice the other man's presence at all, in fact, until he heard a male voice the next aisle over.

"This here?"

"No. These . . ."

"I have those every morning."

"These are much better. See the skin . . . the color . . ."

Dante turned in the aisle, and there was Dominick Greene, talking to Marilyn, flirting over the produce. Greene had dark eyes, high cheekbones, and a sinuous smile. He gave Dante a nod of recognition. In that nod, that smile, the almost familial glance, Dante saw, he thought, the man's insidious intentions.

"We've met," Greene said.

"Yes," Dante said.

"I'm staying close by."

"At the Wong. I know."

"How did you know?" Greene asked.

"My cousin."

"I just came in for some cigarettes."

Greene stuck with them through the cashier and out into the street. He stuck with them to the corner as well. He took some matches from his pocket, lighting his cigarette, and stayed with them down Grant, walking smartly now. He took one pull from his cigarette, then another. His free hand returned to the pocket, jiggling, as if Greene carried something else in that pocket as well. Dante himself carried a retractable blade—the stiletto the cops had missed, with a push mechanism, specially designed.

"Your cousin, he seems to have vanished." The man's voice was sly, hard to read. "I've called him a couple times. He doesn't return."

Marilyn glanced at Dante, waiting perhaps for him to reveal the truth about Gary's death, but Dante said nothing. Greene, he suspected, already knew; the man was playing a game.

"You're in fabrics?"

"Textiles. Italian."

"Made in China, I assume."

"What isn't?"

Greene's eyes were on Marilyn. He had a charming manner as far as it went, and started talking about the new line and its many uses—upholstery, fabrics, women's clothing—and something about that chatter suggested a conversation he'd employed, more than once, to gain the attention of women.

"You've traveled widely," Dante said.

"Not so much."

"Luzon?"

Greene acted as if he did not heard. It was there, in Manila, where the diplomat had been found hanging in his cell. The man's son had been murdered first, though. Then the wife.

"I've noticed you," Greene said to Marilyn. "I've seen you around."

"Oh."

"At Moe's. In the square."

"I grab coffee there, in the morning."

"Dressed for work."

She smiled, flattered. "Yes, I work at Prospero's."

"The real estate firm?"

Dante did not want Greene accompanying them farther.

The man sensed his uneasiness, and was enjoying it in the way some men enjoyed such things, sneaking glances at the other man, flashing him over as he flirted with the girl. Possibly it was only happenstance, their running into Greene: a bored salesman, horny, out for a stroll. There was a challenge in the way the man stood there, hands in his pockets, groin first.

"We get off here."

"Up Union?"

"Yes."

Greene kept his eyes on Marilyn. "Well, I'll see you again," he said.

On the way up, Marilyn sauntered a little more slowly than Dante might have liked. They lingered together on her stoop. A car engine misfired up the hill somewhere. A couple sat talking in a vehicle two houses up, and a woman pulled down a shade across the way. There were small movements in the dark. None of these movements meant anything in and of themselves, but it was only a matter of time. Greene had been in town awhile. If he was with the company, probably he already knew where Marilyn lived. Probably he knew Dante's habits as well. Meanwhile Marilyn was waiting for Dante to say something. Lake had let his feelings be known, and now it was Dante's turn. Still, the thing Marilyn wanted him to say, and the thing Dante needed to say, they were not the same. Instead, he thought of Greene and his silk suit coat and the taunting smile. Dante felt a blind certainty about Greene, the kind of feeling— based in jealousy—that he knew he shouldn't trust, but it was irresistible nonetheless. He and Marilyn kissed, but it was different now, with a message from David Lake flashing on the phone inside, more likely than not, and Greene roaming around out here in the dark.

"What do you want to do?" she asked.

They'd been to this place before, more than once. They'd circled around each other for years. There'd been other men, other women, but there was only so long this kind of thing could go on.

"It's not fair. To any of us."

"There's something else," Dante said.

"What?"

Her eyes glimmered expectantly in the dark. Nearby, parrots cawed in the palms. The cathedral sounded down on the square, its bells muted in the fog. Yet he could not say what he had to say, not now. He touched the stiletto in his pocket.

"The little house," he said. "Tomorrow, I'll come take a look."

She kissed him. It was a sweet kiss, full of promise, and he believed for a moment that everything would turn out all right.

TWENTY

D ante found Greene at the Melody Lounge—a hotel bar adjacent to the Sam Wong Hotel. It was a place where young people came to sit and drink and flirt after work, though that group had pretty much cleared out by this time and it was the hotel crowd now: downscale business travelers and tourists on a budget. There were some locals, too, of course, but there were always locals.

Greene sat drinking. The man's attention was focused a couple seats down the counter on a pair of divorcées, on vacation, judging from the looks of them, midforties, traveling together. They were all laughing it up pretty good. Dante remembered these kinds of moments with the company, waiting. He remembered the hunger hollowing him out.

Dante took the empty seat between Greene and the women. The man's face showed his surprise. "This is a coincidence. Twice in one night."

"Not entirely."

"You're interrupting our conversation."

"It's okay," said the blonde. She was full of cheer. "There are four of us now. We can take a booth."

"You two do that," said Dante. "My friend and I, we'll be along in just a minute."

"I don't believe you." She pouted.

"Maybe they want to be with each other," said her girl-friend. "Maybe they are that kind."

"That's the way it is in this city. So I hear," said the blonde. The women were taunting them now, the pair of them. "How's a girl supposed to have any fun?"

"We'll be along," Dante repeated.

Greene moved to follow, but Dante stopped him with a hand on his forearm. A look of confusion passed over Greene's face, though there was still the smirk and the silk suit coat and the good looks.

"What can I do for you?" he said.

"You've met with my cousin."

"I didn't know you were involved with the warehouse."

What he had to say next, Dante felt as if he were back with homicide, making the same announcement to each new witness, each new suspect, waiting for their reaction. Meanwhile, Greene glanced into his drink. He had a look of naïveté about him, that little-boy look not too different from his cousin's. The dark eyes, almost beseeching, but with that light way down in the center. It could be he was exactly what he presented himself to be: a go-between man trying to figure the best way to bring his goods to port.

"Have you talked to Gary lately?" Dante asked.

"Did he send you?"

"No."

"Then what's your point?"

"I've seen you about a lot lately. Do you usually spend so much time in one port?"

"There are other parties. Other warehouses."

"I can make things a mess for you," Dante said.

"I really don't understand."

"I think you do."

"No."

"Gary's dead."

The polarity in the man's eyes disappeared. They were all black now, with no more reflection. At the same time, though, Greene seemed to shrink into himself, as if he really were the role he played, a two-bit scammer in a silk suit who had nothing to do with the matter at hand. He thrummed his fingers on his cigarette pack.

"I need a smoke."

"I'll go with you."

"I'd rather smoke alone," he said.

"Why?"

"You seem a little off."

"The feeling's mutual."

"The girls are waiting."

"If you don't want to talk, I can go to the police."

"I need a cigarette."

Dante followed Greene outside. If Greene was the businessman he seemed—if he had nothing to do with his cousin's death—he'd turn tail right now, Dante thought. He'd get the hell away from me. His cousin, however, dealt with a lot of people who were on the borderline. So it was possible this man had nothing to do with the company, or with the Wus: that he was an independent operator with whom his cousin had considered making a deal. Dante transferred the stiletto from his jacket pocket to his hand.

They walked down the alley, and Serafina's was just ahead. Dante had been out there the other day, watching Stella's son load the mechanical lift that rose up out of the walk.

"I don't know anything about your cousin," Greene said. "He was recommended to me, that's all."

"For what?"

The man started to talk about his business, something about fabrics, about container size and wholesale distribution patterns, the kind of talk Dante had engaged in himself once upon a time, as part of sting operations, or what masqueraded as such, because as often as not the company was making deals of the sort that facilitated the passage of goods in exchange for certain kinds of information.

There was something disjointed about Greene, something off in the small pinpoint of light way back in his eyes. Dante suspected the man was fucking with him, one way or the other.

"Which one you want?" Greene asked.

"Which one?"

"Inside, the blonde or the brunette. Which one?"

"Neither."

"That's not very nice."

"This isn't about them."

"Then what's it about?"

"You."

"Me? Listen," he said. "It isn't smart for you to talk to the police—you know that as well I do. I talked with your cousin, true, about running some shipments, but there's no use talking about it now. With all the heat, there's no way." Greene threw his cigarette on the ground and put it out with his foot. "I think I am done with this," he said, but stood there nonetheless, as if waiting for Dante to make the first move: to turn around and go ahead of him inside the bar. The man bent down to tie his shoe, taking his time about it, eyes on Dante the whole while.

"Your girl, Marilyn, she's a nice-looking one," the man said. Dante didn't like the sound of her name in his mouth. "She's not the type that stays tucked away, though, is she?"

Dante had seen a picture of the diplomat's wife. A good-looking woman. He remembered how Marlilyn had preened under Greene's attention. There was a softness in the man's menace, something likeable and foolish in the turn of the lips, the sidewise smirk. They were at stalemate now, each waiting for the other to go on ahead.

"Things have changed," Greene said. "Sorry your cousin is dead. Truth is, I didn't need him in the first place. And I don't need you."

A fresh cigarette hung from the man's mouth. He made a move then, jerking his hand down into his pocket. It was a sudden move, like a man stumbling, just clumsiness, too much to drink, but at the same time his eyes gleamed and his lips pulled back into a grin, and there was something deliberate, too deliberate, about the way his hand grasped down into the fabric. Dante pummeled forward. It was an instinctive move. Too late to do anything else. *The shot is coming.* He would take it in the kidney. He drove one palm down, hoping to deflect what was coming, the quick burst of fire out of the man's pocket—and with the other hand he gripped the stiletto. There was an instant when he considered his impulse might be wrong—when he understood there might be no shot coming, when perhaps he could have stopped himself— but then he was already in motion, his hand on the slide button. Whether what happened next was out of volition or the sheer force of the mechanism, or the anger inside himself, the result was the same. The blade sprang out as it hit the man's chest, and he pushed it through in a single thrust, through the rib cage, the cartilage, into the heart. It was something he'd done before, self-defense, but he'd accomplished it too adroitly to doubt his skill in such matters. He had his own training, his own instincts. He pushed Greene into the wall, into a cranny in the brick, legs against legs, staring into his eyes and watching the tiny prick of light fade, glass over, as the man's mouth fell open and his body jerked and then jerked some more and the air hissed out and the fluids gushed. Some people passed at the mouth of the alley, but they kept going, not seeing, or not wanting to see. Thinking what they glimpsed was something else altogether, the way the one man held the other so tight, face-to-face, chest to chest, thrusting him fiercely against the alley wall.

Dante entered Serafina's through the back door, jerking up on the faulty handle Stella had been joking about a few days before. He pushed the button that triggered the lift in the alley, then lowered Greene into the basement. Dante yanked the man's ID and rummaged the pockets. He found a revolver in an ankle holster, but nothing in the pants pockets, only a plastic Bic. It was possible he'd been mistaken about Greene's identity, but the way the man had been hovering, he didn't think so. It would be weeks before the new owners tackled the place, according to Stella. Weeks before anyone found the body. Likely the company would notice the disappearance of an agent before then. When they did, they would come after Dante harder than ever, but at least Marilyn was safe for the time being. He had bought some time. Now he dragged Greene's body off the lift, farther into the cellar darkness, down to where the ceiling dropped and the outline of an old door showed in the trowel work on the concrete wall. Once upon a time, all the basements had been interconnected. A man could crawl through these tunnels. You could make wine in Stella's basement and vanish up through a manhole cover onto Fresno Street. Nevertheless, all those doors were gone, the passageways sealed. Dante went back upstairs. He stripped off his bloody shirt, exchanging it for a clean one in the dishwasher's closet. Then the next morning he took the stiletto and the shirt, and anything else that might incriminate him, and threw it in the Bay.

PART FIVE

TWENTY-ONE

D avid Lake's house stood just off the crest on Sacramento Street, at the outer edges of Pacific Heights. A large house, impeccably kept, freshly painted—a Victorian in a block of Victorians. Lake stood in what earlier times had been called the parlor room, furnished now in a fashion that blended the modern and the antique. He dressed in a nondescript way, but with a tucked-in look— a sandy-haired man who might be called good-looking, though there was at the same time something a bit too pampered. It was tempting to dislike him, except there was a tinge of irony in his manner, as if he had been placed in this position by a hand other than his own. There was also wholesomeness, perhaps, a determination about his features that made one hesitate in such judgment.

Dante had not come alone. The person with him, Jake Cicero, was not someone familiar to Lake: a short man, mid-sixties, in a yellow polo and khaki slacks who looked as if he just stepped out of a tanning salon. David Lake studied them both, not turning away, but Dante's appearance on Lake's doorway, here with Cicero, had taken him aback. Lake and Dante had encountered each other before—on social occasions, on account of Marilyn—and there was an uneasiness between them. Then there was the matter of Dante's trade, an ugly trade, and Lake's suspicion that he himself had been studied and surveiled, his life imagined and re-created by this man in front of him.

But ultimately the reason behind his discomfort was more personal.

They were both in love with the same woman, David Lake and this man in front of him. This investigator with the smell of violence about him. With his long nose, his dark eyes. A face that seemed perpetually hidden in shadow.

D ante had met with Cicero earlier that same day, down at the office of Cicero Investigations. During that meeting, he had sketched out the situation for his boss, but the situation he described, and the reality, did not correspond in all their details. Jake Cicero did not need to know everything. Jake did not need to know, for example, about the dead man Dante had left on the storage room floor beneath the Serafina Café.

"I need to get Marilyn out of town."

"She's involved?"

"No, but I'm worried, just what these people will do."

"What does she know?"

"Nothing. And it would be best to keep it that way. For her to leave—without knowing anything about this."

"What would inspire that?"

"There's a man, David Lake."

"What about him?"

"He proposed to her."

Cicero surveyed the street outside the office window. He did not press Dante, not right away. He knew something of Dante's relationship with Marilyn. He also knew something of the time Dante had spent in New Orleans and the kind of associations lingering in his past.

"You want her to go away with this man, David Lake."

"Yes."

"Your cousin's murder. There's something you're not telling me."

"You won't be aiding a suspect, if that's what you are worried about."

"What makes you think Marilyn will go along with this? You and she . . ."

"Things between us"—he hesitated—"I'll take care of that. I'm more concerned, when she leaves, no one knows where she's gone. Or with whom."

"It will cost money."

"I know."

Dante put an envelope on the table, and inside the envelope there was a good deal of cash. Dante had worked for Cicero for a number of years. They were friends, after a fashion, but friendship went only so far. A different man might have made a show of not wanting the money, but

Cicero was not that way. He'd been in the business for a long time.

"These people, they're dangerous?"

"Yes," said Dante.

"I went to the doctor's office yesterday. For my yearly."

Cicero had used to be pretty slack about his health, but he'd grown more diligent lately, since marrying Louisa.

"What's the verdict?"

"I could live another million years, a heart like mine. So long as I don't fall off a cliff."

Behind Cicero, bocce trophies lined the wall, but Cicero did not play bocce much anymore. It was an old man's sport. His new wife was some twenty years younger than himself, and he had instead taken on a program to keep up with her.

Tennis in the mornings. Diet. A little bit of Grecian Formula for the hair.

Sharper clothes.

A yellow polo open at the collar and a Rolex watch.

Dockers and black loafers, tasseled.

"How is Louisa?"

"She's fine." Cicero thumbed through the cash with an expression of a man caught between two worlds. He was not one to embark on idiot adventures, but on the other hand, Louisa had expensive tastes. Cicero was a fool sometimes, an old fool, but he enjoyed his life.

"This Lake, he's a wealthy man?"

"Yes," said Dante.

Cicero nodded his approval, then turned back to the window, eyeballing the passersby. There weren't any.

"Business is slow?"

"Got a call late yesterday. From a divorcée."

"Same one who was outside the other day, checking our directory?"

"Haven't met her yet. She and her new boyfriend—according to her, the ex-husband is sleeping with the guy's wife."

"It takes all kinds."

"Yeah." He gave Dante a look. "I guess it does."

TWENTY-TWO

Later, Cicero and Dante had taken the drive over to the Victorian in the Heights, and now they stood in the man's living room. Over the past year, Dante had followed Lake on more than one occasion. He had seen Lake and Marilyn walking together and seen, too, the relaxed pace, the easy banter. Dante wanted to tell himself there was no spark between Lake and Marilyn, that this would fade, but he'd seen then—as he saw now—the look in the man's blue eyes.

"This concerns Marilyn?"

"As I explained," said Cicero. "It's a touchy situation."

So far, Dante had let Cicero do the talking. It was possible he could have handled arrangements on his own, but Cicero had a gift that he did not have—a likable smile, a shrug of the shoulders. He wanted Cicero here to diffuse things if the conversation went wrong. Even with Cicero, he worried how Lake might react, especially now, as he described his cousin's death.

"But what does that have to do with me?"

"It's not you we're worried about," said Dante. "It's Marilyn."

"The killer's still out there," said Cicero.

"I don't understand."

Dante could see Lake vacillating, wondering if he had made a mistake, letting them into his house.

"You have to take her out of town," said Dante. "The two of you should go off, immediately."

"We don't mean to alarm you," said Cicero.

"That's exactly what you mean to do."

"You're in love with this woman?"

"I don't see how this is any of your business."

"I've known Marilyn for a long time." Dante saw the flash in the other man's eyes, but he went on regardless. "I know you proposed to her," he said, "I know that." He lowered his voice, as if speaking to a friend, but he and Lake, they were not friends. "She told me, at my apartment. Not so long ago." He didn't need to mention the apartment, but he had wanted to see the small quiver as Lake imagined the two of them, their shadows intertwined in the little place on Fresno Street. The man's uneasiness gave him some small satisfaction, but whatever pleasure Dante took, at the same time, he knew Marilyn had spent time here, in Lake's house. Walking barefoot in her morning clothes along this carpet, up those stairs.

"Just listen," Cicero said. "Then do what you think best."

Dante let Cicero do the talking. It was the same story Dante had told Cicero. Not the truth exactly, but close enough. There were debts, gambling debts. The people who killed his cousin wanted their money, and they had made threats if Dante did not cover those debts. They would go after people close to Dante.

"What about the authorities?"

"The authorities couldn't protect my cousin," Dante said. "They won't be able to protect her."

"I don't like this."

"We are going to need money," Cicero said.

Dante glanced at Jake. This hadn't been part of the plan. Dante had already put the cash on the table, but apparently Cicero wasn't satisfied. Dante knew he shouldn't be surprised, because he'd seen it before, the way Cicero worked a case from both sides, putting the touch on clients at either end.

"You want money, to pay these people off? To get rid of gambling debts?" asked Lake. "Is that why you are coming to me?"

"There are arrangements that need to be made."

"This is blackmail."

"The first thing you need to do is get on your knees and propose," Cicero said. "Then climb on that private jet of yours and fly away. Meantime . . ."

"What?"

"You don't want anyone following. Do you?"

This was the moment, Dante thought. David Lake made a move as if to get out of his seat, as if to end the conversation. Dante did not want him to do this. Because if Lake rose, he would have to stand up and block his way. He would have to find another means of persuasion. He recalled the dead man in the alley and the pleasure he had taken, despite himself, driving the knife into his heart.

"You have to take her away," said Dante.

This next part, too, he left to Jake. The smooth talk, the details of the coming excursion. Jake in his polo shirt and his chinos. Tanned Jake. Golden-tongued Jake. Who made the whole idea seem like a vacation. Who described a little cottage in a faraway place. A plaza with cobbled stones. A chapel.

"Take her on her honeymoon. A long honeymoon. By the time you get back, all this will be over. Meantime, again, there are expenses on my end," Cicero said, "and I will need advance payment."

"What kind of expenses?"

"No one can know that Marilyn has gone off with you. We need to make it look as if she is not with you, but somewhere else. The details, the particulars, I can inform you, if you'd like. Though honestly, it would be better for you to stay in the dark."

David Lake sat with his hands between his legs. He had inherited his parents' money, and then inherited his ex-wife's money when she died. Now Marilyn was being given to him, too. Perhaps he didn't want her this way, but ultimately it didn't matter what he wanted. He seemed to understand this now. There was a hitch, though, Dante knew, and it was not the money. She had not accepted his proposal.

"She loves you." Dante saw the mixed emotions on the man's face, wanting the knowledge, wanting to hear it—but not from Dante. "The thing between me and her, it's just something that happens in the dark."

Lake looked at him with disdain, and Dante realized his mistake, he had pushed it too far. Lake lowered his eyes and said nothing. You should tell me to fuck off, Dante thought. You should be at my throat, a comment like that, with Cicero trying to pull you off. You should be pushing me against the wall, the way I pushed that man in the alley. But Lake didn't do any of these things. A better man for it. Maybe.

"How do I know, soon as we're back in town, this won't start all over?"

Later this afternoon, Dante was supposed to meet with Marilyn, out at the house in Marin. He would prove himself then. He would make sure it was over—but he didn't need to tell this to Lake.

"You'll be married."

"You'll be back, won't you? For more money."

"I don't want your money," said Dante.

Cicero held up his hand. "Let's make it simple. One payment, in advance. Cash. For operational expenses." Cicero smiled—his old-man smile, cherubic, his eyes sparkling—but there was a hardness there, a seriousness, and it was clear he wasn't going to let the matter go.

"Give Jake what he needs," said Dante. "Just do as he says. And let's not talk about this anymore."

D ante and Jake Cicero were in the car now, headed up
over Franklin toward the Broadway Tunnel.

"Is he going to do it?'

"I think so."

"He won't go to the cops?"

"I doubt it."

"Are you sure you can do this?"

"What?"

"Let go of her?"

Dante glanced into the mirror. A car had pulled up behind him. It followed for a few blocks, dropped off. Then
there was another car.

Just cars . . .

He studied them anyway.

"About the money, the way you pressed him?"

"It's business."

"You could have warned me."

"Marriage is expensive," said Cicero.

Dante knew how it was with Jake and his wife. Louisa
liked to shop, and Jake liked to go with her, watching her sift
through the racks, the high-end stores, trying on one outfit
after another. He would touch the clothes before she put
them on, the pleated skirts, the buttons, the blouses, and then
she would model for him, turning in front of the mirror as
he sat in one of those soft chairs, listening to the store music,
while a clerk hovered nearby, expensively dressed, pearls
about her neck, smelling of the store's perfume. The cost of

these outings, and others like them, all the things Lousia liked to do, they added up.

"There's this jacket. Coco Chanel."

"Does she look good in it?"

"Real good. I'll have to call the clerk soon as I get to the office, put it on hold. But I want you to tell me, who are we dealing with here?"

"It's not your concern."

"It might be."

"Make the arrangements. Do it like we discussed."

They had already been through this, and there was no reason to go through it again. Cicero knew a young woman, a criminal investigator who used to work vice and liked to put herself out there. Do her hair, dress her in the right clothes, and she could pass for Marilyn, once the real Marilyn was gone.

A decoy.

It was a touchy business, but Dante didn't need her long. Then she, too, could be on her way.

Dante pulled the car to the curb. Cicero's office was at the top of the hill, but he wanted to be sure no one had followed.

"So you going to make me walk?"

"It's better."

"Yeah, I need the exercise."

"Stay away from me, from here on out. Any communication, we do it by phone."

"I'm already gone," Jake said, but he didn't move. "What if they figure it out? What if they track me down?" A shadow crossed the old man's face. Earlier, Cicero's concerns had been brushed aside by the man's own bravado, by the pile of cash on the table, by the excitement of the job.

"They might insist that I tell them where she is. Or they might want you," said Cicero. Then the smile was back, creasing his leathered cheeks. "They might offer money if I let them know."

"You've got your money."

Cicero laughed. The old Italian laugh. The laugh of a million *paesans*. His smell filled the car. The smell of tobacco and whiskey and shaving cream, of cologne under the arms, all over his gray-haired chest.

Cicero the wise. Cicero the idiot. Cicero, the old fool, in love with his young wife.

"Louisa will look good in the jacket."

"I miss the bocce sometimes. Rolling the ball."

"She's a beautiful woman."

"Yes, she is," he said. "And I'm a lucky man."

"She's a lucky girl."

Dante watched Cicero go on up the hill, trudging, bent over but unstoppable, vigorous and old all at once.

Cicero, the undefeated, who knew better than to look back.

But at the last minute, Cicero paused, turning at the corner, surveying the hill behind him. He put his thumb in the air.

All clear.

Dante fired up the car.

He swung a U-turn and headed for the bridge.

TWENTY-THREE

Sooner or later, you had to leave. Sooner or later, you had to get out. When the old Italians abandoned North Beach—the mold, the leaking houses, the fucking Chinese—this is where they came.

Across the Golden Gate to sunny Marin.

Buying up the earthquake cottages, the vacation shanties, the dairy land with its cows meandering in the yellow grass.

Marilyn wanted him to see the bungalow, the little house on the corner lot with the palms out front and a trellis over the gate. He knew what was on her mind. She wanted out of the Beach, just like those old Italians. The place was a bit farther up the road, but he pulled off early, taking the ramp down into Sausalito. He'd spotted a car lingering in the rearview, tagging him since he left the Beach.

But he was mistaken. The car did not follow.

Dante went into town anyway, just to be sure. He walked under the pepper trees on the main street, past the boutique shops and the chocolatiers and the waterfront houses that had been turned into bed-and-breakfasts. He studied the faces of the passersby, a man slouching on the corner, a middle-aged woman in her Porsche. The woman gave him the once-over, but that's all it was: an attractive woman, well-kept, bored, glancing at a man in the street. He went out to the end of the marina and smoked a cigarette, staring across the Bay at Angel Island and at San Francisco and considered the idea of doing this thing another way. The cigarette tasted awful, but he smoked it anyway, inhaling the black smoke, letting it do its business down there in the soft part of his lungs.

Forget David Lake. Forget the company.

Get Marilyn in the car, and together they would snake down the coast and leave this whole business behind.

Across the border, down into Baja, a little casita in the hot sand, where no one would ever find them.

An idiot dream.

The company would not rest; he knew that.

He smashed the cigarette out on the planking and walked back to the car. It was a new set of tourists now, with the same baffled expressions. The man at the corner still slouched mindlessly, but the woman in the Porsche was long gone. None of them were of any concern, but it did not prevent him from examining the faces. To his mother, he remembered, in her final days, everyone looked suspicious.

Another option was to do nothing at all. To just stand here and feel the breeze.

Do like his father had done. Play it jolly until he disappeared into the abyss.

He drove north, then turned toward Mt. Tamalpais. Following Marilyn's directions. Through a neighborhood that looked like something out of a picture book, all leafy green. Past the shopping center. Around the corner, between the fire station and the park. Little houses with picket fences, set back from the street, sagging asphalt and wild ivy. Turn again on Willow. Then on Redwood. Stop at the corner of Palm and Pepper.

A neighborhood woman stood idly in the front yard across the way. She had skin like milk. The sun was warm but not too warm. The wind blew through the treetops, and the leaves moved as if in slow motion.

A sign pointed to the open house.

PROSPERO REALTY. BROKER'S OPEN. AGENT MARILYN VISCONTI.

There was a princess tree by the fence, and birds-of-paradise grew in wild clumps on either side of the gate. From the end of the walk, Dante saw the couple amble through the screen, onto the porch, with Marilyn just behind. They made a handsome couple, Marilyn's clients: the tall man in his shirtsleeves and his Dockers, sunglasses—Asian maybe, or Chicano, with the Anglo blood mixed in, so the ethnicity was hard to tell. Meanwhile the woman possessed a similar indeterminacy about her, more in her manner than in her looks, both ordinary and exotic at once, a sensuous woman with plump lips and eyes that were a little too bright.

"Dante lives in the Beach," said Marilyn.

"I guess that makes us neighbors, almost." The woman's accent suggested time abroad. She had a way of standing, seductive, less than subtle, leaning against her husband as she spoke. "Though only temporarily."

"Until we get settled," the man explained.

The conversation went on a little more, giving more information than Dante needed. The man in finance, just transferred. The woman painted. No kids yet, but they were curious about the schools, the neighborhood.

The man shook his hand.

"We'll be seeing you," said the woman. The glint in her eyes was almost wholesome.

When they were gone, Marilyn showed Dante around the house. Until recently, she explained, the house had been on the market with another agent, priced too high. Also, the owner's wife had just died, and the owner got emotional when people looked at the place. It might have sold already otherwise, but the earlier interest had come and gone, and the market shifted. The foot traffic was thin, just the neighbors and the agents, the usual flock, the latter leaving their cards spread over the mantel. The owner had let her make some touches, readying the place for sale, and she suspected he might be willing to come down on the price. Meanwhile, Beatrice Prospero was thinking it might be a good idea to have a full-time agent over here, in Marin, on this side of the bridge.

Dante understood. She wanted the house. She wanted him to like it, too.

Marilyn walked him from room to room.

She had staged the house for sale. Clay pots full of flowers. The bed covered with pillows. Lamps on, even though it was daylight, adjusted just so.

The bedroom had double doors that opened onto a yard with pink flagstone and birds-of-paradise.

He had been here a million times.

They stood looking out at the yard. The way the light was, just now, he could not see her scars. Her face was smooth and radiant. But the one eye rolled, just for a moment, cockeyed, at odds with its partner.

"It's nice, don't you think?"

"Your couple, are they interested?"

He had to do it now, the good thing, the thing he had come to do.

Marilyn shrugged. "I don't think so. They're new to the area. In love with San Francisco, the city itself. You know how that goes."

"I know."

She was waiting for him to say something more. They were back to the same precipice, and he thought now, with a sudden resentment, she enjoyed it, teetering back and forth between two men. She did it to get his attention, or because that's the way it was between them, and always had been, company or no company. This time was different. He had to end it.

"Talk to your sugar daddy."

"What?"

"It's what you've always wanted, isn't it? So talk to him."

Dante was surprised at the venom in his voice, how easy it came. "Though, I think, a man like that, he could afford something a little bigger."

They stood side by side at the window, and he felt her going cold beside him, arms folded, lost to him, almost. He did not look at her. Maybe he could do it another way, more tender, more good, but tenderness, this kind of situation, it never convinced anyone. Still, I need another word, he thought, another gesture. Then the rest of it will happen of its own accord. Lake will meet her after work, with his flowers, his ring, his earnest proposal. She will look at Lake and realize what happened last night between us, on the boat, was just a last fling, that she is, in fact, in love with David Lake. Or that's the way she will tell it to herself later, no matter what she's feeling now, here, arms folded, standing in the bedroom.

"It doesn't matter." Dante felt the nastiness rise in his throat. "I'm willing to play it both ways, if that's what you want."

"What do you mean?"

"You can live with him here—a place like this. Then come over and see me. A little boat ride, any time you're bored."

"You bastard," she said.

He grabbed her by the shoulders then, surprised again at his own vehemence, face-to-face, taking her by the collar. Her good eye was downcast, but the other one, it stayed fixed. "Look at me," he said. He curled his lips in disgust. Whore. Trollop. Marry that other son of a bitch. He searched for some final insult, something obscene and unspeakable, but it didn't come out. Meanwhile the bad eye, the dead eye, the all-seeing eye, it played across his face.

"You're going to tear my blouse," she said.

He let her go.

She stood against the wall, in the shadows, but the shadows had lost their tenderness and didn't hide anything anymore. He saw the suture lines, the mask falling apart.

He walked outside.

The light was bright and idyllic. He started his car and drove back the way he had come.

He glanced in the rearview.

The road was empty behind him.

TWENTY-FOUR

Back in North Beach, the streets were crammed with ghosts. His cousin wandered down Telegraph Hill. Dominick Greene came up from the basement beneath the Serafina Café, lingering with all the other dead, there at the counter. The old Italians wandered with the Chinamen on Grant Street and Dante wandered through them all. Overhead, the light still burned behind the slatted doors in the chambers of Love Wu. Dante inhabited the periphery of Portsmouth Square, studying that light and the Empress Building itself, watching the comings and goings, and for an instant he was up behind those shades, looking down, and in that instant he knew everthing that was going to happen, and he saw Marilyn, too, emerging onto the square, wandering with the dead.

But no. Marilyn had escaped. She was safe. She had met with Lake, and he had gotten on his knees. Lake had spirited her away, to parts unknown.

This had to be so, because Dante had done what he'd needed to do, in the bedroom of that little house with the flagstone patio.

He had done it, the good thing.

TWENTY-FIVE

The next morning, according to plan, Dante drove to Marilyn's apartment. The new woman should be there by now, the one Cicero had hired. Meanwhile, up the hill, the fog had started to part, and a couple stood at the crest, peering through the white mist toward the Bay. Tourists, judging from the looks of them. A big man, strongly built. A woman. Both in Windbreakers and sunglasses. Fresh from walking the Filbert Steps, or Coit Tower. Pausing to catch their breaths and contemplate the view. Dante thought they looked familiar, but dismissed the notion at first, because there were always tourists on top of the hill, and they always had about them something familiar. Then they came toward him, and he saw they were the couple he had met at Marilyn's open house out in Marin.

"Imagine this," the woman said.

"You caught us," said the man. "Playing tourist in our new city."

"You probably take it for granted."

"I do."

"We're taking a day off from house hunting."

It seemed too much the coincidence. The man had a camera about his neck, true, but there was the slightest hesitation in his step, and Dante wondered if they knew Marilyn lived here—if they intended on stopping by. People shopping for real estate could be demanding, he knew. They violated all boundaries. Then something passed between the man and the woman. "Nice to see you," the man said. Whatever their intentions had been, they sauntered on.

The woman smiled over her shoulder.

Watching them, how they meandered down the street, arm in arm, cooing over their guidebook, he could not help feeling there was something wrong about them, how they gushed and fluttered, something off-key. But he let it go. Who was he to know about such things?

Dante went up the stairs to Marilyn's apartment. The woman who answered the door wore her dark hair under a scarf, as Marilyn sometimes did. She wore leggings and a loose blouse, untucked, so it fell over her hips, in a fashion Marilyn herself sometimes wore. At first glance, glimpsing her through the side window as she'd approached the door, Dante had thought she was Marilyn and that everything had gone awry, his plan had fallen through, but he was mistaken. She was a younger woman, the decoy, as Cicero had said she would be. Her complex-

ion was more fair, and her eyes were a different shade altogether.

"Come in. I'm just getting packed." She spoke familiarly,
as if they had known each other for a long time. "The outfit,
I pulled it from her rack."

"I see that."

"Does it work?"

"From a distance."

"I'm too thin. Aren't I?"

She turned on her heels, showing herself. A movement a
dancer might make, though not quite so graceful.

"A little."

"The right outfit. It'll thicken me up."

He followed her up to the bedroom. As it turned out, she
had been through Marilyn's wardrobe, and clothes lay scattered over the bed.

"Marilyn and Lake—did they get off?"

"Yes."

"You're sure?"

"I was at the restaurant, a couple tables over." She paused to
see how much detail he wanted. Dante did not want any, not
really. He could imagine it easy enough: the little scene down
at Romano's restaurant, the candles and the wine, Lake gazing
across at Marilyn, the good man, with his earnest, whirlwind
plan, his desire to take her away, his promise to be gentle and
kind. "You followed them?"

"They spent the night at his place. Then this morning,
they stopped here, just for a moment. She came out with a
bag, not much."

The woman slid off her shoes. Marilyn's shoes.

"I followed them to the airport."

"Was there anyone else?"

"Just the two of them."

"Following, I mean. Surveillance?"

"I don't believe so."

The woman pulled off her blouse and put on a long sweatshirt, tucking the end down into her tights. She was thinner than Marilyn, a bit taller, less voluptuous, but not without her own attributes. She put the blouse on over the sweatshirt—a loose-fitting blouse that flared below the waist. Then she yanked up a print skirt, running her hands over her midriff, flattening and smoothing, tugging at the flare. She put on a wide belt.

"Is this better?"

"Yes."

"Not too fat?"

"No."

She settled in front of the vanity, working her face, brushing the lashes, painting the brows. She worked from a picture of Marilyn tucked into the mirror frame in front of her. Her arrival here had been figured out in advance. Dante had given his key to Marilyn's apartment to Cicero, that last day in his office, and Cicero had given it to this woman. Then this morning, after Lake and Marilyn had gone to the airport, the woman had let herself in.

Meanwhile, Dante had bought a pair of airline tickets.

"I used to work vice, undercover," she said.

"Cicero told me."

"I can make myself look like anyone."

"I don't know your name."

"Call me Marilyn. That's the idea, isn't it?"

"Yes."

"You might as well start now, Dante."

She put on the contacts, changing the color of her eyes, then dipped her hand into the jewelry box—long fingers, slender, not Marilyn's hand, but the gesture was one he recognized, the way she held the earrings up, regarding herself, face toward the mirror. It stirred something in him he did not want to think about. They were an older pair of earrings, something he had given Marilyn years ago. She had been wearing them, too, that evening out at the boat.

"Did you get the identification?"

"Of course."

She pulled a wallet from a purse, one of Marilyn's purses, borrowed from the closet. She handed him the driver's license and stood close to him as he examined it, so that he felt her arm brush against his, the soft sleeve of her blouse, Marilyn's blouse, rustling against his arm, and he smelled, too, her perfume, Marilyn's perfume, heavier than Marilyn wore it.

"It's a good resemblance, yes."

The plan was a simple one, really. Now that the real Marilyn had eloped, gone away with David Lake, this woman would leave, too, only going in a different direction, traveling under Marilyn's name. Despite all the fuss at security these days, all you needed, still, was a boarding pass and a driver's license. If you knew the right people, securing identification was no more difficult now than it had ever been. Cicero had managed it, using Marilyn's name and a picture of this woman in front of him, with her hair dyed and darkened, as she wore it now—a convincing job, not cheap—and the eyes colored in by computer. Her chin was a little sharper then Marilyn's, but all in all, the resemblance was close. She went on packing, using one of Marilyn's suitcases, mingling her things with Marilyn's.

"The universals are mine—but I need a few of her things, signature items, just in case. She did not take a whole lot with her, actually. And anyway, we are close enough in size."

The woman pulled out some lingerie—a lace nightgown. It was a sheer piece of material, gauze white, and the way she held it up to herself just now reminded him of Marilyn and her white dress.

"Do you really need that?"

"Just in case, Dante."

"In case of what?"

"Use my name."

"In case of what, Marilyn?"

She smiled, slyly, pleased at his shyness, at his embarrassment—something a little cruel, perhaps, in the way she turned from him now, folding the lingerie into the suitcase. "This is about illusion," she said. "The illusion, I believe, is that Marilyn is going away. And Dante will join her in a few days."

The way they had planned it, Dante had bought two tickets, one in Marilyn's name, departing today, and the other in his own name, for departure a few days hence. As far as the company was concerned, his goal—he wanted to give the agency the impression that he had decided to clear out, sending Marilyn on ahead.

The woman modeled a string of pearls now, holding them against her collar.

"Not those."

"Why not?"

"They belonged to her mother."

"Everything will be returned."

"Leave the pearls."

Dante carried her suitcase down the stairs, out to the car. A neighbor waved from across the way, and that was a good thing, for them to be seen, headed out like this, Dante and Marilyn.

At the end of the block, the tourist couple sat drinking coffee at an iron table that Old Man Liguria had set out in front of his grocery. It was the same pair Dante had seen earlier, out on the walk, but if they were aware of him now, as he pulled around the corner, they made no sign. In a little while, though, a gray sedan appeared on the road behind him. The sedan lingered in the traffic past Geary, into Hayes Valley.

The plan called for this woman to fly south to Long Beach, then take the ferry over from San Pedro to Catalina Island. Once there, in the hotel, her instructions were to make her presence known, out by the pool, in the lobby. When she was done, she could hang out the DO NOT DISTURB sign. Then, for all practical purposes, disappear.

"Your face," she said, "it's like a postcard."

"What do you mean?"

"A nose like that, you could be on a postage stamp."

"I haven't heard that before."

"Turn here."

"I know the way."

"We're running late."

Somewhere on the freeway, he noticed the sedan again, showing up in his rearview, close one moment, then farther back.

A single occupant, a man. Not close enough for Dante to see.

He slowed to let it pass—to get a look at the driver—but the car slowed, too. Close to the airport, it vanished down an access road, snaking away.

Inside the terminal, they made a show of it.

He kissed her and they embraced.

Himself and this woman he didn't know.

Her eyes were half-shut, and she brushed his lips with her open mouth. The first kiss was innocent, almost, but the second was not that way. Her touch stirred a desire he knew would not be satisfied. Marilyn and Lake had left just at dawn and would be somewhere over the Eastern seaboard by now, edging toward the Atlantic, onward to Paris, or Barcelona, or Rome, the exact destination he did not know, nor

did Cicero. That had been the idea, for it to remain secret—
for Lake to choose the place and keep it to himself.

"At the hotel, make your presence known, but you don't
want to linger."

"You worrying about me now?"

"I just want you to understand. The situation is not without risk."

Her assignment, the way it worked, after she checked in
as Marilyn, the first two days, she would make an appearance or two, in costume, keep up the game. After that, she
was free to disappear.

"I'm going to Ensenada," she said.

"You don't have to tell me that."

"You get tired of this game, you can join me."

"You'll be back."

"Sure, I'll take off these clothes. I'll do my hair. But
there's no reason I have to come back here."

She was toying with him. Holding on to his belt now,
leaning in for one more kiss. It was gentle but not so gentle:
a soft kiss, openmouthed, that smeared across his lips. He
looked into those half-slanted eyes. They were Marilyn's
shades, Marilyn's earrings. Marilyn's perfume mixed with the
scent of this woman, and he imagined for a second that he
might join her in Ensenada. He might cross the border and
let all this go. He touched her again. He put his hand on her
waist now, letting it drift, almost, wanting under those layers.
He smelled the ocean. He felt the hot sand under his feet.
He saw Marilyn in her white dress, out in a plaza somewhere,

in that picture how she wanted it to be. He touched her some more.

"That's good, Dante," she said.

He watched her go down the causeway, toward security. At the last minute, she turned and waved.

But it was wrong.

The way she waved, how she reached, the little flap of the hand, it didn't look like Marilyn at all.

In a vinyl chair, against the airport wall, sat a man in a suit coat. The man was not a traveler. He wore sunglasses and sat with a magazine in his lap, head tilted as if reading, though, in fact, he was looking forward through his dark shades at the couple saying good-bye.

Dante had not seen him, the man knew. Or not recognized him, anyway, as involved as he had been with the woman at the security gate.

Earlier, the man had dressed in a blue Windbreaker. He'd had a camera around his neck and wandered down the hill, his travel companion by his side, and together they had sat with the tourist guidebook there at the Liguria Bakery, drinking the hot espresso. Then Dante had driven by. At that point, the man left his traveling companion behind, walking briskly to the gray car. Following.

Now he stood up.

He had already bought a ticket, the cheapest fare, not caring about the destination, because he did not intend to use it. He needed the boarding pass only to get through security. He followed the woman with the dark hair and the hoop earrings and the wide belt, her hips swinging under the print skirt. She waited at the Long Beach gate, and he waited, too, until after she boarded, to be sure this was her flight. Then he made his call. It would have been a pleasure to pursue her himself, but the woman was not his job, not now. She belonged to someone on the other end. Meanwhile, he had his own work to do. And his companion was waiting.

TWENTY-SIX

Dante walked down along the west side of Portsmouth Square, in front of Cookie Picetti's old place, where the cops and the city hall people had used to eat in the old days, just around the corner from the morgue. There was a rice parlor there now, and an empty storefront next to that, and across the way stood a hotel, from which only the day before the paramedics had wheeled an old woman who dropped dead on the interior stairs.

He surveyed the hotel more carefully. In the front window stood a crowd of Buddhas, all shapes and sizes, large and small, exorbitantly priced.

A man lurked behind the counter, bored as hell.

There were places like this all over Chinatown, selling imitation jade, statues of the divinity in obscene positions. There was nothing much in there a tourist would want, or anyone else, for that matter.

A front, he guessed, for laundering money.

If you examined the books, they'd tell you the statues had been bought cheap, wholesale, for next to nothing. Then sold to tourists, paid for in cash. Except, of course, the books were a lie. No one ever bought the statues. The money that passed through the store, it was drug money. And the statues were thrown in the bay.

He went inside and paid for the room.

He circled the Benevolent Association. Steam hissed up beneath the grate at his feet. There was a light on up top, behind the slatted shades. Love Wu, with his ancient library, full of secret papers. If the mayor was right, Ru Shen's diary was up there. Dante hung in the square, as he'd been doing these past days, surveying the building, watching the come-and-go. Tomorrow, he would check the manifest at the Chinese Historical Society.

Now he headed back through the blue light, down Stockton. The vegetable stalls were not yet closed, and a woman sold moon cakes on the corner. Pigeons fluttered in the alley. Back in the tenements there was a squalling, as of an animal being butchered. A group of tourists walked relentlessly forward in search of the wharf. Dante went on toward Fresno Street. He would have to clear out soon. He touched his nose. He ran his fingers over the long bump and felt the slope of his nose drooping infinitely downward. There was a small buzz at the center of his forehead.

The faintest whisper.

I am already dead.

TWENTY-SEVEN

The Lady in Blue, wearing no blue whatsoever. Chin the impeccable. She'd grown up around the corner and navigated the street as a child, no doubt, with its shadows and its crooked light. Dante regarded her from the darkness of his father's porch, in her patrol flats and gray suit, her pencil skirt and white blouse. If not for the blouse, its white sheen in the dark, he might not have seen her coming up the alley. There was a reason cops wore blue. It made for less of a target at night, when the hard business went down.

Chin, the unimpeachable.

Out all hours, forever on the job. She lived on Mt. Davidson, where the sky was perpetually overcast, in one of those buildings, those lines of condos, that circled the hill at the top of the city. San Francisco was not a big town, its boundaries confined by the Bay on one side and the ocean on the other, and those sprawling suburbs to the south. Physically there was only so much space, the people lived crammed up close, the fog skittering overhead, the blue sky forever about to reveal itself, almost visible, up above the slipping clouds. Chin had lived all her life in the city, same as himself, walking these streets. People talked. She lived alone, and there were rumors about her on this account. About her sexuality, her private life. People in San Francisco did not care about such things, supposedly, but that was nonsense, because who you slept with, everyone cared about that.

The rumor was, Chin slept with no one.

Chin the Lonely.

Cold fish, out of water.

Last duck on the pond.

It explained the late hours, the attention to detail, why all these years she'd dressed in the colors of a cop on duty. Lately, though, she blushed her cheeks, however faintly, put some pencil about the eye, however slight, and sometimes wore a blouse with fluted sleeves. The change had come with her promotion, people said. She wanted to move to the next level, so she had finally learned. You had to be attractive to someone.

"Excuse the hour."

"I'm awake."

"Just a few questions."

"You don't sleep?"

"Loose ends."

"OK."

"Inside would be better."

She had come alone, no backup in the wings, no trace of

Angelo and his boys. This meant she had come to talk, not to arrest him, though that could change quickly enough. He wondered if Angelo knew about this visit. When they were partners, Dante had learned there were times when it was best not to have him along. Angelo had a tendency to go upstairs, over your head, at the first chance he got, and to do so in surreptitious ways. Over the years, his ex-partner had developed contacts with the Feds, inside the Bureau, and a case like this, who knew whom he might pull in.

Inside, boxes were scattered much as they had been during Chin's last visit, only more so. The house was in disarray, and did not give the best of impressions.

"Going somewhere?"

"Just sorting. Between the robbery, and your warrant boys—it's hard to keep up."

"Sorting?"

"Yes."

"You were down to the bank yesterday. You cleaned out your account. And your girlfriend—her place is dark."

It was what he had wanted, for the word to spread, for people to think he and Marilyn were leaving town. Even so, it disarmed him how quickly Chin had followed the thread.

"Where are you going?"

"Everyone gets a vacation."

"The way it looks to me, you don't plan on coming back."

"San Francisco is my home."

"They'll come after you, you know that. Same as they went after your cousin."

"They?"

Chin's eyes were pale gray. He had noticed that paleness before, and noticed the emptiness in her expression—in the flat line of her lips, in the brow. It was tempting to think that this emptiness contained knowledge. That she knew things she was not saying, though he understood this was not necessarily so. It was the mark of a good investigator: the ability to look as if you knew something when, in fact, you knew nothing at all.

Chin reached then into the pocket of her blazer. She had some photos, like last time, but these photos, they were not of his cousin. At least not the one on top, anyway, the one she flipped first. Rather it was a young woman, exposed from the chest up. Dante recognized her. A big-breasted young woman, dark-skinned, standing on a tabletop, her blouse undone, wearing short pants, very short, very tight. It was a portfolio photo of a certain sort, for a certain type of work.

"Do you know this woman?"

"She works at Gino's. She's a dancer."

"A dancer?"

"Yes."

"In what capacity do you know her?"

"In the capacity you might expect."

"You've been asking after her quite a bit lately. Down at Gino's."

"You in vice now?"

It was possible someone had filed a missing persons report on the girl, but Dante didn't think so—strippers came and went—and anyway, that kind of report would not end up with Chin. Dante had not mentioned the girl to Chin in their earlier conversation. Apparently, she had retraced his steps that night, and had probably been retracing other things as well.

"Where did you go with her?"

"When?"

"The night of the robbery."

He had been up to the hotel, of course, to the Sam Wong, but he wasn't going to tell her this, or anything about the company. It would not be wise. Regardless, he could sense her determination, and he almost trusted her.

Chin the dogged. Chin the pure.

"We just stepped outside for a little bit."

"Did you get a room?"

"You don't have to go anywhere special to have sex. You know that."

"Where did you go?"

"Out in the alley. You want the details? Or should I leave it to your imagination?"

"You have been back to look for her several times. You've been over to her residence. You've been down to Gino's. Why?"

"I have a crush on her."

It was a childish thing to say, though in some odd way, perhaps it was true. Meanwhile, the equanimity was still there in Chin's face, but it had a different surface, as if carved from stone, and her eyes darkened. She leaned back, reaching into the blazer again, to the inside pocket, putting the picture away, pulling another. As she did so, Dante saw her holster, and the thin outline of her breast under the white blouse. She held the picture facedown, like a card, on the table.

"What did you and your cousin talk about?"

"I believe we've been over this."

"You didn't tell me everything."

"I told you what I know," he lied.

"His wife, Viola."

"What about her?"

"We released your cousin's body to her yesterday, for the funeral. And I spent some time talking with Viola. She was a little more cooperative this time around."

Dante had forgotten about Viola. After the murder, Angelo and Chin had dragged her downtown, behind the glass window, and apparently the young widow had had some kind of fit. Viola was a redhead who wore her skirts tight and her boots high. She had a very sweet face, and a sweeter figure, but she was barely twenty-seven and prone to hysterics.

"She mentioned your cousin, he'd developed some new associations shortly before he was killed. And I was wondering if you know anything about these."

Dante wondered how much Chin knew about Dominick Greene—if his corpse had been discovered, and if this discovery was what had brought Chin knocking.

"According to Viola, Gary met with a woman."

"He always met with women."

"Viola said, this one, it might have been business."

"It was always business, those flings of his."

"Viola was suspicious, too. But this fling—if that's what she was—this woman, she had an associate. A man. The two of them, she said, what Gary told her, the pair of them worked together. Viola didn't necessarily believe him."

"Do you have a description?"

"Viola saw the woman from a distance, leaving their house—a couple of days before your cousin was killed. She had her hair up, in a twist. A brunette."

"That could be anyone."

"I know."

"The man?"

"No. Viola didn't see him. Viola thinks he never existed. That Gary made him up, to cover the affair."

"It's possible," Dante said. "It's the kind of thing he might do."

"Your family warehouse—the Wus have brought shipments through there on a routine basis, we are sure of it. And your cousin got a cut."

"I'm not in the family business."

"Who employed you, while you were in New Orleans?"

Straitlaced Chin. The little girl who had grown up around the corner. Who'd seen her own uncle shot to death in the Chinatown restaurant. Who looked, despite everything, like a girl in the uniform of the Salesian school. The earrings, the makeup—none of that changed anything. She was the sort who pieced things together. She worked in SI; she had access to records.

"This investigation, I get close," she said, "and people are killed, witnesses disappear. Files get pulled."

Her face remained placid. Her brows were a flat line over her eyes, and she sat very straight and still, stonelike, ancient, but at the same time, he could see the alertness, her lips trembling, the quickening of her breath. She understood, he thought. Like that statue in Yin's office, facing every direction all at once, a multitude of outstretched hands, each of them empty, holding nothing. The truth wasn't one thing but many. Not just the company, the Wus, the police, each a separate entity moving of its own accord, snakelike, but all moving at the same time, intertwined, so it was impossible to separate one from the other, to penetrate to the core of it, to eliminate your own desire, your past. *Ru Shen*. He wondered how much Chin knew.

The moment passed. She was just a cop, sitting there.

"There's something else," she said. "Your cousin, he told Viola, these people—they told him you had something they wanted."

"What might that be?"

"I was hoping you might have that information."

"My cousin had money problems," he said, "but I told him there was nothing I could do."

Chin knew he was holding back, but he could not tell her about the journal even if he wanted to. She was working with Angelo, and the department was a sieve, information traveled, so if he spoke to one, he spoke to the many, and there were people among the many he could not trust.

Chin flipped the second picture, the unplayed card.

It was a woman in a vinyl jacket, head twisted. Her body was in the early stages of decay. A gash festered at her neck and the tongue protruded from her mouth. It was the same girl, the prostitute from Gino's, in the same vinyl jacket.

"Forensics says she'd been lying in an alley, maybe a week. In an abandoned area, not far from where she was living."

Chin could take him downtown, even charge him, given the similarities to his cousin's death, but if she had meant to do that, she would not have come like this, alone.

"There's a pattern here," said Chin. She was right. First his cousin, now the girl—though exactly how the pattern would repeat . . .

"I told you before," she said. "I can help you. You can't do this alone."

He had the impulse then, despite himself, to tell her everything, and the suspicion, as well, that she already knew. But then something about her changed, in her eyes, in the turn of her mouth, and he saw, however fleetingly, that girl on the street corner struggling to make sense of things, and he realized Chin, too, was lost in the maze.

"Who's next?" She tapped the photograph. "That's the question I want you to ask yourself."

"I've told you everything I know."

She resumed her old posture, unreadable. "If something else occurs to you, let me know."

"I'll think about it," he said.

"Don't think long."

TWENTY-EIGHT

A million eyes roamed the streets of Chinatown. A millions hands. A million feet. Yet no one saw him. Or seemed to see. Their eyes rolled over the produce. Hands touched and squeezed. The old ones in their shapeless clothes, their two-dollar shoes, they stepped aside, but they did not see him, white ghost, all but invisible. They had learned the trick of this, the lesson, passed on long ago, by those who had survived. The Anglos, the Euros—they were not real. If you did not look at them, if you did not see them, if your eyes did not meet their eyes, then they could not hurt you. The younger Chinese, in their sharp clothes, it was the same thing, only different. For them, it was not a matter of superstition. They did not see him, because he was unimportant. The white man, he did not exist.

The clerk at the Chinese Historical Society fulfilled his request without speaking, guiding him to Special Collections, where he could examine the manifest. The list describing the objects in the collection contained only the most cursory of information, but he found Ru Shen's name there, in the itemization of artifacts for "Across the Water." It was a list of Chinese characters alongside English transliterations:

孺 神: Ru Shen. Diary of unknown stowaway.

Dante spent some time with the transliteration guides. The ideogram at the top of the entry was simply Ru Shen's name, as written in Chinese. Then there was the symbol at the end of the line:

It took him a while to find its meaning—but it turned out to be a scepter, a ceremonial staff: a symbol of good luck, or of evil, depending upon the nature of the mind that perceived it:

"As one wishes."

TWENTY-NINE

Dante climbed into his Honda and headed south. He left the freeway in San Bruno, then pulled into a place called the New Airport Suites, just off the freeway. The place was neither here nor there, just a complex of buildings, remodeled stucco, with nothing to recommend it other than its proximity to the airport. He had chosen it because of the way the buildings sprawled haphazardly across the lot, with multiple exits, which would make his comings and goings hard to watch.

It was possible that the company had already replaced Greene. Or that there'd been someone else watching all along.

He checked into the hotel, though he stayed only long enough to see if another vehicle had followed him. Then he left. His cousin's funeral was later this same day, just down the road in Colma. He needed first, though, to visit the surplus store down on El Camino, stocked with supplies for survivalists: men who liked to play soldiers in the woods, with Mylar vests and paintballs and exploding cans of smoke. The owner also sold guns under the counter.

Dante had a plan.

Later, he would return to the city, but he could not stay on Fresno Street anymore. After the funeral, he would come back to the New Airport Suites, but he would not stay the night here either. Instead he would drive the car into the airport lot. He would go through security, as if he were boarding the plane, but then he would come back out again. He would go through a series of maneuvers to make it look as if he were leaving town, then go back to Chinatown, to the nameless hotel. Inside the surplus store, he bought what he needed.

The Italian Cemetery was up in Colma. The usual thing was to have a Mass out at Saints Peter and Paul, in Washington Square. Even the families who no longer lived in the neighborhood often held the viewing down in the Beach, at the Green Street Mortuary. Afterward, the funeral cars would wind through the streets of the city, ending out in Colma. That was how it had been when Dante's mother passed, and his father, too, and his uncle as well.

Viola had forgone all that.

His cousin's assets had been frozen, and she had little money. So she held the service at Caputo's Memorial, not far from the cemetery itself. If the service had been held in North Beach, it would have been better attended. There would have been the old-timers from the Beach, but there would also have been more gawkers, drawn by the murder.

As it was, there were only a handful in attendance, including Viola and her kids, and Nancy, too, the first wife.

The two women were not on speaking terms.

His cousin's burial plot stood down in the oldest part of the cemetery, not far from SFO. The freeway passed on either side, and there was the roar of jet engines overhead. The air tasted of fuel. This part of the cemetery was laid out in concentric circles, the gravel road spiraling through the outer fringes of the old Italian cemetery, through the lonely and crumbling stones toward the inner, more desirable plots. Past the old-lady cannery workers who'd lost their fingers in cans of Del Monte peaches. Past Nick Abruzzi, who'd killed his brother's wife and hanged himself in prison. Past the giant stone fish, a memorial to fishermen and shipwrecked sailors. Past the aged widows with no markers at all, and the restaurant workers and dock laborers all lying in long anonymous lines that reached from here to the end of time.

Down to the family plot. To his mother and Grandfather Pelicanos. To Salvatore Mancuso and Regina. Down there among Avincenza and Tony and Jojo and all the dead relatives whose names were forgotten until you stood among the stones.

The way the graveyard had been laid out, circles within circles, it gave the effect, no matter where you stood, that you had found your way to the center: a hole in the black earth, six feet deep, with the dirt mounded alongside.

Viola lurched toward him, all in black but for her purple

scarf dangling wildly. Her makeup was smeared. The way she approached, he thought they might find some mutual consolation. He wanted to speak with her—after the ceremony— about the people she had described to Chin. Viola stumbled on her heels. He reached to steady her.

She gripped his arm fiercely and pushed her face into his. "This is your fault," she hissed. "You fucking asshole. You could've helped him. You could've done something."

"Those people, the couple . . ."

"Now I'm destitute. The cops are going to take every goddamn cent."

"I'm sorry."

She slapped him, making a show of it, the way she brought her hand back, swinging wide. He could have stopped her, he could have grabbed her by the arm, but he did not want to get into it with Viola, wrestling next to his cousin's grave. The priest, his mouth fell open, and one of the kids started to weep, the family closing around the boy, but they'd all, Dante suspected, taken some vicarious pleasure in her action. Viola stepped away from the others, beautiful, alone, petulant. When the ceremony ended, the priest put his hand on her shoulder, but she would have none of that. She shrugged him off and went stomping through the stones.

D ante departed the cemetery, shoulders slack, his long face even longer now. He peered past the gravestones, surveying the road as he walked, the figures on the horizon. A man with a shovel. More mourners. A woman placing flowers on a distant grave. Viola was right: His cousin might still be alive if not for his own involvement with the company, but there was little he could do. His cell vibrated in his pocket. On the small screen, he discovered a text message from Jake Cicero.

Meet me at the office. ASAP

It was unlike Cicero. Jake did not send text messages, but rather had an aversion to the whole concept, his fingers too fat and wide, his eyesight too dim, his patience too short to navigate the tiny keyboard. Besides, today was Monday, Jake's tennis day, and every Monday afternoon he went down in his shorts and his polo shirt to meet Louisa at the club. If Jake's life were only Jake's, if it were only Jake and Jake alone, the man might not leave his office except to eat and drink. That's the way it had been for a while, between wives, but things were different now. Dante didn't think Jake would skip out on Louisa.

Dante left the path. He stood among the older graves where the earth had settled, and dialed Jake's cell phone. There was no answer. He tried the office landline, but that call went unanswered as well.

THIRTY

Cicero's office was at the crest of the hill, on an abut-
ment overtop the Broadway Tunnel—in a building
that trembled with the traffic rumbling below.
Dante wheeled into the parking terrace, on the south side,
and pulled in alongside Cicero's sportster. On the front seat
sat a box from Coco's on Union, wrapped with a giant yellow bow. Apparently Cicero meant to surprise Louisa later
this evening, after they'd finished on the court.

Dante could not imagine Jake wanting to meet him tonight. And he could not imagine him sending a text as op-
posed to picking up the phone.

Even so, Dante went up.

It might not be the wisest thing, but if something had
gone wrong—with Marilyn and Lake, with the decoy—he
needed to know. Or if Cicero needed his help . . .

The office was on the third story, at the end of the hall.
The outer door had been stenciled in the old fashion, black

letters on rippled glass. As a rule, Cicero left the door unlocked when he was inside working, but not tonight. Dante used his key. Then he pushed the door open, standing back as he did so, knowing that if there were anyone here—anyone other than Cicero—the real trouble would come now. Cicero's office was toward the back, past the receptionist's desk, and his door stood partly open.

"Jake!"

He called the name a second time, but he already knew Jake wasn't going to answer. Maybe it was the smell, not a strong smell, but a smell with which Dante was not unfamiliar, a vague aroma, like stale clothes too long in the back of a car—a sickly smell, like that of a man who sweats too much, whose perspiration smells faintly of urine and blood. A smell that a nose such as his own—oversized, absurd in its dimensions—was uniquely suited to detect. Though perhaps, too, the odor, the rising certainty, was simply the scent of fear rising from his own skin: the suspicion he'd had from the beginning that things would turn out this way. He'd been selfish, putting his old friend at risk.

When he walked around the corner into Jake's office, the smell was less subtle. He could smell the blood; he could smell the shit. A fly buzzed. A lazy fly, circling slowly. Descending with its thousand eyes. Coming to light on the tiny flap of skin on Jake's neck, rubbing its front legs in the open wound.

Jake had been garroted, strangled while sitting down in his oak chair, the one that swiveled. His back was to the window. The blinds were closed.

Dante understood his mistake. He'd been wrong about Greene. Cicero had been garroted in the same fashion as the others. So Greene was not the murderer, Greene could not have killed Cicero, because Greene himself was already dead, lying in the basement of the Serafina Café.

Dante thought of the prostitute and her contradictory stories regarding who had recruited her. He thought of the story Viola had told Chin, about the man and the woman who'd contacted his cousin. And he thought, too, of the couple he'd seen on the hill outside Marilyn's house.

Greene had not been the agent after all.

Dante examined Cicero's office. There was nothing in the appointment pad. He punched the button on the answering machine and listened to Louisa's voice, asking for Jake to call, sounding a little tipsy, a little pissed. The club they belonged to, out in the Avenues, had a bar courtside, and there were times she and Jake never made it to the court, lingering at the bar instead. Dante glanced over at his partner, who sat with his head wrenched back against the window blind. Then he dialed Louisa.

Louisa did not sound thrilled to hear from him.

"Have you seen my husband?"

"No, I haven't." Dante turned away from the corpse. "He's not answering his cell."

"Big surprise. He never answers his cell. I've left half a dozen messages."

"Did he say anything, earlier?"

"What's going on?"

"Did he have any appointments, that he mentioned?"

"Some kind of divorce business, I don't know. Some couple—he was going to meet them at the office, but that was hours ago."

Dante glanced at his partner again. The fly had burrowed itself into the wound in such a way that it looked like a black mole on Cicero's neck.

"I'm sure he's on his way."

"That man, you know, he makes a big deal out of where I go, who I see, suspicious as can be. But where is he now, that's what I want to know?"

"He was down to Union Square earlier," Dante said.

"Union Square?" Her voice rose.

Union Square was the shopping district, downtown. Dante remembered Cicero talking about Louisa and her thighs, how she looked in her white tennis shorts. It was embarrassing, a man talking about his wife like that, but Cicero could not help himself. She loved looking at herself in the mirror, changing clothes, this outfit, that, and Jake, he loved to lie on the bed, watching.

"He was picking something up," said Dante.

"For me?"

"I think so."

"Well . . ."

He heard a sweetness then in her husky voice, mixed in with a greed she could not help. *The thing I love about Louisa,* Jake had told him, *the thing I can't resist, that girl, she's always out for herself.*

In the background, a man laughed too loudly, one of their tennis buddies, those guys who got under Jake's skin, the way they flirted with Louisa. It didn't mater now. Louisa would get it all. The little condo, and the sports car, and the membership at the club. She would close out the office, cancel the lease. Maybe I should tell her, Dante thought. Maybe it would be easier that way, if she heard it from someone she knew. Nevertheless, he could not get involved with the police, not now. Rather, he needed to clean up after himself, wipe off the prints, do his best to leave without being seen. The body would be found soon enough. Then Louisa could do whatever it was Cicero feared she might do—find another man, younger, who'd drive around in the little silver car and spend all the money Cicero had never got to spend. Never mind, though. Jake would be a saint in her book.

Lucky girl.

"He's on his way, I bet."

"I'm sure."

"He probably just got caught in traffic."

"Do you want me to leave him a message?" she asked.

"No. I'll catch him later."

Dante got off the phone.

He left the building, but he had not gone far when he received another text on his phone.

We have Marilyn.

PART SIX

THIRTY-ONE

Dante lay naked on the bed, inside the nameless hotel, with the revolver on his chest. After leaving Jake, he'd driven to the motel in San Bruno, as planned, then circled back to Chinatown. Now, lying on the bed, listening, he could not escape the feeling he had been here before. The pigeons fluttered at the window, pecking at the rotting sill, as if there were something delectable hidden beneath the paint. Another one of the birds flew in, chest puffed, pushing for its place. The noise rising from the street was meaningless, chaotic. There was the sound of laugher, guttural Chinese, coughing and hacking, of voices calling across the square, and of a rally truck returning. Evangelists, or the supporters of Ching Lee, the mayoral candidate who was challenging the incumbent.

The polls had tightened as the race entered its final week, with Ching Lee hammering Edwards from one side and Gennae Rossi pounding from the other.

Dante's ears were acute. Too acute. Hearing things that weren't there. The rustling of a dress. The old Cantonese, at the far end of the alley, meditating, muttering a Zen koan in the back of his throat.

He dialed Jake's phone, thinking those who'd stolen it, who'd left the earlier message, perhaps they would answer. But it was just Jake's voice, prerecorded, full of ash and whiskey.

They had found Marilyn. Or her double in Ensenada.

The wise thing to do, perhaps, was to wait. To sit tight until the company called, except he knew what they wanted, and he had grown weary of waiting. He went to the closet. The apartment smelled of the previous tenant, the old woman, but her scent was stronger here, where her dresses dangled and her skirts drooped, hanging on metal hangers: half-buttoned blouses, frayed sweaters, old skirts, stylish once but too frayed now even for the salvation stores in the lower Mission. Alongside the dresses hung a canvas bag. He took the bag from its hook and put inside a can he'd bought at the surplus store in San Bruno. The can held a particular kind of phosphorus, white phosphorus, which had particular kinds of uses.

He put on his clothes and stood looking down into the alley.

It was nice to think you had a choice, that your actions made a difference one way or another, that you could somehow change things. He liked to think this was true. Meanwhile, the fire alley ended in a blind, and the iron gate at the other end was locked. He took the staircase down to what had once been the central lobby. The lobby served as a storefront now. The old hotel counter was more or less intact, and the clerk sat on the other side of the counter, near a fat Buddha whose hand rested in an unseemly place.

The store was full of large statues, imitation jade priced as if it were the real thing. The goddess Para. The Buddha sublime. Siddhartha under the Bodhi tree. Some of the poses were quite classic at first glance, but there was nonetheless something titillating and askew. An erection beneath the robes. A lecherous grin.

Guan Yin, goddess of compassion, her ass up in the air.

The counter man had a thin mustache and nodded at Dante. He was not Chinese, but Russian, and it was the Russians, Dante knew, who laundered money in shops like these, ledgering cash receipts. Even so, the place ultimately answered to the Wus, most likely, but that was true of most every business in the area.

"The iron gate," said Dante. "At the top of the alley. You keep it locked."

"You have a problem?"

"That's a fire alley."

"Tell the fire marshal, you don't like it." The clerk was surly, but at the same time, how he shifted, eyes darting, it was clear the fire marshal was the last person he wanted involved. With the election going on, and the hydrant failures, the bad press, a code violation could shut the place down. "The homeless, you leave that gate open, they defecate all over the alley."

"It just makes me nervous, that's all."

"I don't like their shit in the alley."

"The old Chinaman—he has a key. . . ."

"He keeps the alley clean."

"So you let him sleep there in return?"

The man was uncomfortable. Dante took out his wallet and put some money on the counter.

"You must have another copy."

"What do you want it for?"

"In case of an emergency. I'll just sleep a little better, if I know there's another way out."

Dante smiled. The clerk looked at the money.

In reality, Dante wasn't worried about fire. Rather he was looking ahead, in the event he returned to the hotel and needed a quick avenue out. In a pinch, he could climb the escapes at the end of the blind, but the gate would be better.

The clerk took the cash and reached under the counter. The Russian handed him the key, and Dante had a premonition then, or something like a premonition: a feeling, similar to the one earlier—as if he had been here before. As if he were looking at himself from some other point in time.

But it was an illusion. He was here now, alive. The room was full of Buddhas. On the other side of the counter, the Russian grinned unpleasantly.

"I'll be back," Dante said.

Then he pushed outside, through the door, into the unceasing noise.

THIRTY-TWO

Nelson Yin had habits, predictable to a degree. So far as Dante could tell, Yin left the Benevolent Association after work at almost the same time every afternoon, at which point he would go in one of two directions: either to the garage underneath Plymouth Square, or to the Golden Dragon. If he went to the garage, this meant Yin would be driving home in his blue Nissan, to his wife and family on the peninsula. If he walked the other way, toward the Dragon, he would linger there for an hour or so, drinking and dining with his associates. On those days, he returned afterward into the upper reaches of the building.

Dante sat in a restaurant across the way, in a window booth that offered a view of the Benevolent Association, waiting for Yin to emerge. No one seemed to be paying any mind. Dante knew how to blend in, so that people who looked at him, they did not think twice. He had become skilled at this during his days with the company. This invisibility was a little more difficult close to home. Then, too, there was the matter of his nose. The fisherman face of his grandfather, beak like a pelican, a knife edge for gutting the belly of a fish. The family nose. Ridiculous. Too large for his face. It kept growing, after the rest of you stopped. And kept growing even in the grave.

He sat in the window, the newspaper in front of him, a cup of tea, noodles with watery broth and gristled meat.

Finally Nelson Yin appeared.

Yin hesitated on the sidewalk, as if he himself did not know which of the two ways he intended to go. It would be best, so far as Dante was concerned, if Yin headed home—if he stepped into the crosswalk and tramped toward his car in the garage beneath the square. Then Yin would not get in the way, and Dante would have just a little more time.

Yin strutted instead to the Golden Dragon.

Dante finished his tea. Then he gathered his satchel, with the canister inside, and ambled across the road.

D ante could not gain access to the upper floors through the Wus' lobby. There was too much security. So for Dante, the only way up lay through the Golden Dragon. The restaurant sprawled on the ground floor of the Empress Building, an ornate place with an intricate floor plan, full of crooks and turns, booths with high walls and backroom tables, areas within areas, separated one from the other by painted screens. At the back, near the kitchen, a staircase rose to the upper floors, but even then access would not be easy.

Yin had entered before him and already joined another party: two men who sat drinking at a table on the far side. At least Dante would not have to walk past Yin to get to the stairs.

The hostess was dressed in silk with gold leaf.

"A booth, please," Dante said. "On this side."

The hostess studied Dante and the small canvas sack in his hand, but there was nothing remarkable about the sack itself, or about his presence, other than the fact he did not much resemble their usual clientele.

"You are only one person. The counter would be better."

"I have more coming."

"Reservations?"

"No, I'm sorry."

"Let me check what's available."

Dante listened to the murmur of the place, the after-work crowd, tired people growing animated with food and drink: Chinese real estate agents and money-traders, clerks and chiropractors, dental technicians and legal aides. Some of them rented space in the building and did business with the Wus, but the lines between legitmate business and not-so legitimate, these were always murky.

The hostess put down her list. "How many?"

"Four. Plus me."

She frowned. "One minute."

A man at Yin's table gave a glance in his direction, but it was cursory, meaningless, and Yin himself faced the other direction. Dante did not wait for the hostess to return. He headed toward the kitchen, then turned at the half wall, past the restrooms, toward the stairs. He had been in the Dragon years ago, and the fundamental layout had not changed. At the top, the stairs opened into an adjacent structure that had been added to the original building in the twenties, and from there he could make his way over. The stairs were carpeted, and pictures had been hung along the wall: pigtailed men in front of the Chinatown Mercantile; a Chinese crooner; still shots from the Chinese parade; men in business suits, men like Nelson Yin, harmless on the surface of it, pudgy at the middle, bland smiles, colorless eyes.

Halfway up, Dante pulled the canister from the satchel. He could see down over the half wall into the restaurant, where the hostess moved in her gold leaf and the patrons leaned over their drinks, and he could hear, too, the clatter of dishes and the murmur of the customers over their plates. He held the canister between his hands. Except for the mechanism at the top, the small pull-ring and the chain, it was an unremarkable canister, of the type that might be mistaken for a quart of paint or a tin of tomatoes. The can, of course, contained neither of these things. Rather it contained the white phosphorus, a chemical composition that ignited with exposure to air.

Dante hesitated. There was no guarantee Ru Shen's journal was in the building. Even if he meant to go upstairs, this distraction he was about to create might cause the opposite effect. Instead of buying time, he would draw attention. There could be unintended consequences, but he had been over this already.

He pulled the ring.

Then he tossed the device underhand, a single, easy motion, as if throwing a softball at a family gathering. The canister bounced once at the bottom of the stairs; then it went off, the phosphorus catching fire as the can burst open, a brilliant yellow flame. The smoke came pouring out, a thick white smoke that billowed from the can and kept on billowing. Dante spun toward the door at the top of the stairs. Meanwhile, the smoke filled the room behind him. He could hear people bolt for the exits, gagging and hollering. The alarm was ringing, and in another instant, the elevators would shut down. As Dante headed up, workers from the uppers floors brushed past him on the staircase, coming from the opposite direction, hurrying down.

THIRTY-THREE

The Empress was not one building but several, its wings built at different times, intertwined and honeycombed with passages. The staircase up from the Dragon went past the fifth floor, then ended abruptly, halfway up the next flight, in a blank wall. Dante had hoped to take it all the way up, then cross over to the Benevolent Association, but the staircase was sealed, apparently, to secure the upper floors. Down a landing, back the other way, down a passage leading to the Association, he encountered a locked door. So he went down a short corridor, to the corner where the buildings joined. Outside the window there was a maintenance ladder embedded in the stone, giving access to the roof. A few days before, on surveillance, Dante had seen the ladder from beneath and now stared down the long shaft in the other direction, at two men loading vegetables onto a sidewalk lift far below. The men did not look up. Dante hoisted himself onto the window ledge, grabbed the nearest rung, and climbed hand over hand on the iron bars until he reached the next floor.

He swung awkwardly across the chasm.

Yin's office was down the hall, unoccupied. The floor had been abandoned. The main elevator was shut down, on account of the alarms. The cargo lift to the top floor, however, still operated, creaky and slow as it might be, chiming steadily as he rode up, then chiming once more, louder, more definitively, when the lift bumped to a stop. He jammed the lift door behind him, propping it open, so the lift could not be called from below. He did not want anyone to follow.

A hall led away from the lift, a nondescript passage, olive-colored walls lined with shelving, household goods, all labeled in Chinese: bags of rice, paper towels, boxes of hard candy, medical supplies, catheters, a bundle of adult diapers. The alarm was still audible, though only faintly, ringing many stories below. The hall had a sour smell, more pronounced as he continued on. He heard, too, a whirring nose, as of an electronic device, like a motor turning. The old woman appeared then, in her wheelchair at the other end of the hall, wearing a silk robe that hung loosely, too loosely, so he could see, the closer she came, parts of her anatomy he did not necessarily want to see. She lifted her hand from the controls, and the machine halted sideways in the corridor. The old woman squinted at him as he approached. She regarded him with skepticism but no particular fear. An oxygen bottle dangled at the side of the wheelchair, poorly attached, and tubing ran from the bottle to a mask that hung from the old woman's chin.

"There's a fire downstairs," he said.

"Nelson sent you?"

Dante said nothing.

"Nelson called. Not me, of course, the other one, his sweetie. He told us to stay put. He would come himself. But they are not letting anyone into the building."

"That's wise."

"But you got by."

"I did."

"Nelson sent you?"

"Yes."

The woman grunted. She nodded toward a cluster of portable tanks jammed up against the shelving. Her manner suggested she was used to giving instructions, and also to being obeyed.

"I need a tank. This one's almost empty."

Dante picked up one of the oxygen bottles and followed her into the main apartment. Close by, next to the old woman, the smell reminded him of the smell of his room, back at the nameless hotel, only more pungent. The woman appeared to be in the midst of some project. The table spilled over with magazines, catalogs, old books, and the floor nearby was littered with torn paper. Whatever she was doing, she resumed now. She picked some scissors from the pocket of her wheelchair, cutting and jagging along the edges of a colored picture. Dante set the tank down. He could see from the gauge that the current tank was running low, and he could also see that the woman was short of breath, but despite her trouble breathing, she handled the scissors with a singular ferocity, and it looked as if she had been at it for some time. The trail of torn paper led back across the floor to a cluttered alcove. A door stood open farther on, and on the other side, Dante could hear the sound of a younger woman, humming, moving about, pushing hangers in a closet. Her footsteps approached, then moved away, padded, soft, unhurried.

"She thinks she's somebody else, my nurse. Or so she would like to think. It is the trouble with young women." The old woman bent over her work as she spoke, so it was unclear to him whether she was speaking to him or to one of the people in her colored picture. It was a singsong voice, make-believe, such as that of a mother addressing her children, or a child speaking with paper dolls. As she continued, her English trailed into Chinese. The padded footsteps came closer now, without warning. Then the young nurse stepped around the corner.

Dante's brow was sweaty with the exertion, his body damp, his clothes disarranged. In some ways, he did not much resemble the figure who'd appeared in Yin's office several days before, but he saw immediately that the nurse recognized him, as he did her. She looked into his face, at the large nose, and her expression was the same as it had been that day in the lobby, only now mixed with her disdain and her porcelain beauty, there was a touch of fear. The fear, it widened her eyes, and this widening, it made her more beautiful. She wore the same cheongsam blouse, and her face had been carefully made up. She carried with her the scent of perfume, a tincture of lilac.

"Nelson sent me," he said.

The old woman barked in Chinese. From the way the nurse reacted, and the glance between them, Dante guessed the old woman had said something about his presence. The old woman was mad, no doubt, but only half-mad, not so gullible as she seemed. She was shrewd, a little shaky but strong in the upper arms, the way she spun the wheelchair about all of a sudden.

"Air!" she demanded.

Dante nodded his OK, giving permission for the nurse to help the woman, but at the same time put his hands on his hips in a manner that let her see the holster under his jacket. In this way, this gesture, he was not so different from his friend Angelo. Or from Chin.

"You do not come here to help us," said the old woman.

"This is your library?" He nodded toward the alcove.

"You do not work for Nelson," the old woman said. "You are not police. You are not fire."

"There is a journal, by a man named Ru Shen."

The young woman took a step backward, the slightest step. His guess, the nurse was not American-born Chinese. Unlike Yin, she spoke both languages, same as the old woman.

"The things back there, they are from the old days." The old woman glanced at the trail of paper along the floor that led to the darkened alcove. Her glance was not without longing. On the table closer by were stacks of magazines from the new China. "But there is a fashion industry in China," the old woman said. "Many new things. Someone has to keep track."

Though it was midday, the chambers were dim and cloistered. The balcony doors were shuttered, with the blinds at
half-slant, and there was no breeze. From what he could see,
the old woman slept in the room in which they stood, on an
adjustable bed in the corner, and there was a small kitchen
beyond. The remaining room, from which the nurse had
emerged, just past the alcove, was nicer, more carefully furnished, sparser: A large bed stood at the center of the far
wall, covered with an intricate silk spread. This room had
its own bathroom and an armoire and a vanity against the
other wall. Like the young woman, the room smelled as if it
had been tinctured with lilac.

Dante stood on the threshold of that room. There was a
door at the far end. He would have thought it a closet, except for a dead bolt that latched from the inside.

He unlatched the bolt and peered down a flight of stairs
into the darkness.

"What's this?"

"For emergency."

Like the others, the nurse did not look at him when he
spoke. Maybe because she was lying or maybe out of habit.
Because a woman in Chinatown did not meet the eyes of a
white man passing on the street, let alone those of a stranger
appearing in her bedroom.

"Where does it go?"

"No one uses it anymore."

Dante remembered the sound of her footsteps ascending
behind the wall of Yin's office. He had a pretty good idea
where those stairs originated. Dante studied her carefully

made-up face. Though her eyes darted away, he studied it anyway. He did not want to get rough with her, but there was only so much time. On the floor, a pair of men's shoes sat by the armoire. He walked back over to where she stood, there on the threshold.

"Lock the wheels," said Dante.

"Pardon?"

"I don't want her rolling around."

"I don't understand."

"Yes, you do. The wheels have a lock, down low, where the patient cannot reach. So she does not roll herself into oblivion."

The young woman did as she was told. Dante smelled again the sour smell he'd noticed in the hall, and realized it came from the old woman, the smell of urine and perfume mixed together.

"Ru Shen," he repeated. "His diary—it's here."

"I am just a nurse. I don't know anything about it."

"On your knees."

He did not much like the tone of his voice. He heard cruelty and also a joy inside that cruelty. He bound her wrists behind her back, wrapping them with duct tape. Then he pushed her down on her stomach, face to the floor, and wrapped her ankles. It was for her own good, so she would not be roaming around while he examined the library.

"Nelson will kill you for this," the old woman said. "With his bare hands."

He saw the thin smile on the old woman's face, however,

her lips pursed out. The crone enjoyed the spectacle of the young woman lying bound at her feet. She did not much care for her young nurse, and the nurse, he suspected, did not much care for her.

The alcove smelled of paper and dust. The boxes were stacked to the wall, and the shelves were piled with old ledgers, full of Chinese characters, shipments in and out, pages yellow with age, ripped and torn, but from the looks of them, the ledgers had been preserved by happenstance more than anything else. The shelves were poorly arranged. There were boxes of pictures and more pictures, photographs— relatives, he'd thought at first, but there were too many for that—and there were envelopes, too, of figures carefully clipped from their surroundings.

Dante could see there had been a logic to it once, scrap-books of the woman's life, pictures of herself, friends, pages from letters and journals, arranged according to the events of her life, the world around her—but at some point, the woman had lost focus.

Along the bottom shelves, yet more. Children's books. A Chinese encyclopedia. A history of silk. Schoolgirl diaries. All of which had been clipped as well, pages removed, dog-eared, sullied, smeared and scribbled, the books themselves filed according to a plan no longer decipherable. Then, against the wall, boxes and more boxes. He went through these, too. In the bottom tier, he found the boxes he'd hoped to find, or so they appeared to be, labeled along the top with the address of the San Francisco Library, and containing more catalogs, collector's items, some of them from an older time period but now ravaged: items he recognized from the file list of "Across the Water." He rummaged through them, book by book. The old woman had taken them for herself, clipped and pasted, integrated them into her world. But if Ru Shen's journal had been among the artifacts, it was here no longer.

From the other room, all of a sudden, came a tinny sound, oddly muffled, that reminded him of the Chinese music boxes the shopkeepers used to sell along Stockton Street. He stepped into the main chambers, but there was no music box. The old woman sat in her wheelchair, and the nurse lay on the floor, her face in the carpet. The refrain ended, started again. Dante kneeled over the nurse. Her blouse was loose, and her slacks stopped just below the knees. She stiffened as he searched her, but he did not stop, instead running his hands over her until he found the cell phone in the waist pocket of the cheongsam.

The ringtone ended, started again. He flipped open the cell and looked at the yellow screen.

Nelson Yin.

No doubt there was a scene out on the street: fire trucks and squad cars and tourists with cameras. Among these would be the patrons from the Dragon, Yin among them. He had called on his cell, concerned about his lover's safety. Dante went to the slatted shades. His temptation was to step onto the balcony, to peer down into the street and get a good look at the action below—but if he did so, someone in the square would notice. There would be a stir at the sight of the unknown man appearing on the balcony of Love Wu.

Dante thought about the hidden stairs, the locked passages, the secret passage up, and glanced again at the girl.

He widened the slats and stood there as he had once imagined Teng Wu standing. Dante listened for the whispering of the men down in the square, for the crackling of the magnolia leaves and the sound of the sampan in the Bay, for the sound of the tunnels being dug and the tracks being laid and the short-handled hoe hitting dirt and the pickax in the goldfield and the wheels of the fishmonger's cart rolling down Grant. Of the dice rolling in the brothel. Hearing, too, the rustling of a white dress in a square far away and a squad car door shutting and heels clicking in the alley. His own name whispered. Scissors clipping. Behind him, the young woman grunted on the floor. He had felt the softness of her clothing, the warmth beneath, as he had searched her, looking for the phone.

The nurse knows, he thought.

She is Yin's lover and she knows, and I have wasted valuable time. He touched his gun, wondering how far he would have to go to get her to speak. Then there was the possibility, too, that the journal was not here at all.

"Come here," said the old woman.

"Why?"

"I want to show you something."

The old woman had managed to reach one of the scrapbooks stacked on the table nearby, an older one assembled years ago, in which the inner logic had not yet deteriorated, its outer cover emblazoned with the symbol of the Wu family. Inside the book were pictures of this room as it had been in the past, and of a Chinese man, very old, and others who had lived here once upon a time. "That is me as a little girl," she said. "I was from a good family. They sent me here by clipper, and I never saw them again. They wrote me, though. Teng's wife was old, and he was old, too. I nursed them both." The woman did not say much else, but he understood, looking at the pictures, that she had been more than a nurse. She had been mistress to Teng Wu, or Teng Wu's son—it didn't matter, it was impossible, ultimately, to tell them apart, and they were all dead now. When she had gotten too old, her place had been taken by a younger woman, who herself had gotten old, but these others, they were all dead now, no trace, only these pictures clipped and scattered, and now there was just her, living with this nurse of her own.

Except this young woman, lying on the floor, was not like her. She had come from that new China, and Nelson Yin, he went back and forth from the suburbs, and all the pictures and letters were all meaningless now.

So this is what is left of Teng Wu's library, he thought.

"Nelson pulled some strings," the old woman said. "He got these for me. Missing pieces. Lost relatives."

The old woman gestured at the recent clippings. These were older pictures, and Dante realized the source. They had come from the historical exhibit, "Across the Water," secured so that the old woman would have more pictures for her endless project. *Ru Shen,* he thought, and something came clear to him, almost, but then the phone rang again. Dante went to the woman on the floor.

"Speak in English," he said. "Tell him everything is okay. That there is no hurry."

He flipped open the phone and held it so the woman could speak to Yin. She did as she was told. The conversation did not go on very long, but Dante worried Yin would notice the fear in her voice.

He heard at the same time a noise in the corridor below, as of footsteps ascending.

"Where is he?"

"He is going home to his wife."

Dante realized, no, with this woman waiting, so soft to the touch—with her wide eyes, her childlike pout . . . No, Nelson Yin had not gone home to his wife. Yin knew the building well. Yin could get past the firemen easily enough if he wanted. He undoubtedly had access to that locked passage on the other side of the blocked stairwell. It also occurred to Dante that the man had called his mistress not from below, but from inside, as he climbed up the hidden stairwell. Then, as if to verify his suspicion, there came more clearly the sound of ascending footsteps in the wall behind the adjoining room, and of keys now, rattling in the bolted door. The old woman fell silent and the younger woman on the floor lay still. They realized, too, what was happening. It was Yin, on the other side of that door, opening it now, in the bedroom, calling out his lover's name as he came across the floor.

"Pi Lo."

The young woman stirred, as if to respond, but saw the gun in Dante's hand, and out of wisdom, or self-preservation, or the paralysis of fear, she checked her impulse. At that moment, Yin appeared at the threshold, a Chinese businessman in his dust-colored suit, his red tie, a bead of perspiration on his forehead, exhausted from climbing the stairs. His eyes met Dante's, darting from him to his sweetheart on the floor. Something transpired between them then—himself and the nurse and Yin—or so Dante imagined. The so-called blind hunch, communicated not by logic but by the flashing of the eyes, the wrinkling of the brow, the kind of thing that did not stand up in a court of law, but which was revealed in the circumstance of the moment. Ru Shen's journal had been stashed away in the historical society, unread, forgotten, just as the mayor said. It had been brought here, with the other items, a plaything for the old woman, a distraction, discovered, perhaps, by the young woman, thumbing through the articles in the box. The nurse had shown it to Yin, and whatever was inside, Yin had decided to make use of it. Blackmail—of whom, exactly, Dante did not know—but he had seen the mask fall away from Yin that day in his office, the desire underneath—just as he saw now the look of a man undone by his foolishness, realizing he had been found out, though by what mechanism, exactly, Yin could not know. Yin raised a hand in confusion, wanting to know, perhaps, why it was this particular man who had found him, but there was something else in his expression as well, a quickening. Dante heard the old woman fussing behind him, but he did not turn his head. He focused on Yin. He stepped forward. Behind him, the old woman lunged. She was strong, despite everything. Aiming at the small of his back, he would think later. At his kidneys. But Dante had already started in motion, so the arc of her arm as it came down, the descending thrust, entered lower than she intended. Still, it was a good thrust. She jabbed the scissors deep into his thigh.

In that instant, Yin bolted back the way he had come.

Dante felt the pain, as of something tearing inside, his leg giving way, but this did not prevent his reaction. He came around with his right elbow, knocking the old woman in the face. Then stumbled toward the threshold. He propped himself against the door frame lest his leg give way. If Yin had not closed the stairwell door behind him earlier on his way inside . . . if that door were open now . . . if he had attacked Dante instead of running at the instant the old woman thrust the scissors into his leg . . . then things might have been different. As it was, Yin had to pause to open the door. He flung it open recklessly, at the top of the stairs, but that small delay was too much.

Dante fired once.

The bullet caught Yin in the back. The man staggered into the stairwell and went tumbling down.

There was an ugly noise down in the stairwell. Dante pulled the scissors from his leg.

The young woman lay with her head to the ground, sob-bing. Meanwhile the old woman cried in a muttering, hopeless kind of way. Her face was bruised, and she had lost her oxygen mask in the scuffle.

"Help me," she rasped.

The nurse wriggled on the floor. Dante kneeled over her, but he could not hold the squat. It was too painful. His first thought had been the wound was superficial, but it did not feel that way.

"Ru Shen . . . ," he said. "I want the journal."

"I don't know anything about it," said the nurse.

The old woman was gasping, only there was, as in everything the crone did, an aura of the theatrical. She struggled for air, and her hands clawed for the mask. She could not reach it. Dante cut the tape from the nurse's hands and feet, unbinding her. He watched as the nurse reattached the tubing, but at the last moment yanked the oxygen mask from her hand.

"To the lift."

Po Li wheeled the old woman down the narrow hall toward the lift. Dante had jammed the lift door on his way up, and now he cut the electrical wire to the control box. Then he lashed the door shut, so they could not get out and cause him any more trouble. Meanwhile, the old Chinese woman gasped, not blue yet, not quite, though she would be soon. Her throat spasmed and her chest began to heave.

"The journal."

Dante pointed the gun at the young woman. She was young and beautiful, but at the moment he did not care. Then he dropped the sight, as if to shoot her in the leg and maim her for life.

"It's in Nelson's office," the woman said.

"Where?"

"On the shelves, maybe. Or in his desk. I'm not sure."

"If it's not there, I'll come back."

"It's there."

"Are you sure?"

She nodded then. The old woman let out a fearful whine. He felt the pain in his leg and was tempted to shoot the old woman in such a way that it would take her a long time to die. Dante threw the mask inside the elevator, then went through the bedroom and down the stairs. Nelson Yin lay sprawled at the bottom. His body heaved and gurgled unpleasantly, but it was just the after-death stuff. The internal organs discharged themselves in a long hiss that smelled of the sewer. Meanwhile, Yin still held the keys to the passage in his hand. Dante pried them loose, then stepped over the man's body. The staircase kept going, but there was another passage to the right, and he walked through the darkness toward a thin light at the bottom of a door up ahead.

When he pushed open the door, he found himself in Yin's office.

Dante went first to the bookcase, to the old books, and he hurtled them off one by one. They were fragile, loosely bound, ancient, but this was not his concern.

There was noise out in the hall, and he could hear the main elevator coming up the shaft. The rescuers were on their way.

He went into Yin's desk then.

He yanked open the drawers.

It was a businessman's desk, and down in the bottom

drawer, on the left side, he found it, underneath a stack of papers.

Inside the journal there were more papers, notes, written in a different hand. He gathered them all, then descended into the stairwell, taking the dark passage down.

THIRTY-FOUR

The taxi wound out of Chinatown, South of Market, past the streaming lights of the Moscone Center. It had been skid row here, not one block but a dozen, a tangle of old hotels and rooming houses, the old South Beach neighborhood, once full of watch parlors and fix-up shops and cheap housing for the dockworkers, the Blue Blocks so-called, on account of this was where the bus from San Quentin dropped of its parolees, in their blue denim pants, fifteen bucks in their wallets. The Blue Blocks had been plowed under and paved for the conventioneers and the hotels. There was a park now, concrete, a shopping complex lit by panes of colored light, but the denizens had not vanished, only scattered, living in the cracks between the warehouses and the lofts and the new bars and the seed joints and ecstasy clubs and old Victorians gone to hell amid empty lots full of rubble.

The taxi turned on Brannan, then turned again.

To a cluster, a freeway underpass, ten lanes wide. The traffic thundered overhead. Sagging buildings along the noisy street, under the steel abutments. Lean-tos made of corrugated tin, carts of stinking clothes. A liquor store and an auto repair shop on the bottom floor with rooms overhead, rented by the night. Across the way, a gentlemen's club, so-called, a half-trendy place where a cluster of young women lingered on the corner.

"Here," Dante said.

The taxi stopped. Dante had been here a few days back, looking for the girl from Gino's, not expecting to find her, but this wasn't why he was here now. He had come because the way to the nameless hotel had been blocked with men and equipment. During the taxi ride, the pain in his leg had not abated. He looked at the women at the corner, then down into the darkness of the freeway underpass. The area was fenced, but this did not stop anyone from making it over. Hooded men, solitary, waiting. Perched behind these, at a distance, groups of milling boys. Then, scattered around, in the shadows of the concrete abutments, other figures, hunched, prone, lying in a field of burnt tinfoil.

The pain in his leg was bearable, almost, but there was another pain that was not. He had been places like this before, in his other life. Or places close enough. He had not wanted to end up here, but part of him had expected he would and yearned for it nonetheless.

"Do you want me to wait?"

"No," Dante said.

The taxi drove away.

Dante had caught the taxi on Leavenworth, several blocks up from the Wu Benevolent Association. So far as he knew, the driver had not noticed his leg, though the man dealt with all kinds of clientele and did not look like the sort who cared about much other than his fare. After he was gone, Dante went across to the liquor store and took out his wallet to pay the clerk for a room upstairs, in the quarters overhead.

"Identification?"

"Why?"

"Listen. I don't care, but if the cops swing through here—and they ask to see the register—if I got nothing on paper, they might go room to room just for fun."

Dante gave the man his driver's license and watched as he wrote down the number. It was a fake license and a fake number, but Dante knew it didn't matter much either way. The cops rarely came down here, and those who did were bullyboys who shook down the junkies for extra cash. He also bought a bottle of Jack and some cigarettes and a container of ibuprofen. The TV hung in the corner above the counter, reporting on the incident at Plymouth Square, drumming it up. Billowing smoke. Panic at the thought of fire.

"No smoking," the clerk said.

Upstairs, Dante lit up anyway. He drank the whiskey and lay down with the gun on his stomach. Unlike the nameless hotel, this place had a name, at least according to the receipt, but it wasn't a name worth remembering. The place was down a step from the nameless, the rooms smaller and dirtier, and the neighbors less wholesome. He cleaned his wound and disinfected it with the whiskey: a puncture wound, dirty scissors—it already bloomed red in an ugly way. He peered out the window at the figures beneath the freeway. He knew what they sold back there and he was tempted; ibuprofen got you only so far. Meanwhile, across the way, a young woman standing apart from the other prostitutes beckoned the passing cars. A driver slowed. Brazen and shy at the same time, the way she leaned into the window. She might have reminded him of the dead girl, the dancer from Gino's, only the stance was all wrong, the sway of the hips. His days with the company, fresh from some assignment, he'd found solace in places like this—back in those shadows. The prostitute looked in his direction but didn't see him. She climbed into the john's car and was gone.

The mattress was old, the sheets stained. The streetlamp burned furiously just above the window, and the thin curtains did little to block the light. The noise from the freeway was constant. You had to be drunk to fall asleep here, or high. Meanwhile his leg hurt. A dull throbbing that got worse as the night went on.

He stripped off his bloody pants, but the room was cold, and so he put them back on.

He finally fell asleep, sometime after three, but it didn't last long, because then the morning traffic rumbled over the freeway. The road's concrete buttresses rose on either side of the hotel, so close the vibration seemed to emanate from the building itself. Sometime later that morning the traffic herded to a crawl, idling, a throbbing hum, an impatient sound with a great nothingness at its core.

He lay listening to that nothingness in the sound. He thought of the old Cantonese behind the nameless hotel, in the lotus position, meditating. At some point, he entered that sound himself and maybe he slept. Maybe that was what you called it. When he opened his eyes again, it was midmorning. The room was filled with a purgatorial light.

He spent most of his day in his room, tending to the leg. It was stiff. He staggered up the street with some difficulty and bought some three-dollar trousers at the thrift store. They did not fit well, but at least they were reasonably clean. He took some more ibuprofen for the pain and drank some more whiskey, but it didn't do any good.

Under the freeway, the figures moved in the gray light, the dealers standing alone, runners in back, users hunched and lying about like so much debris. Whores wandered on and off the corner.

Dante felt the pain in his leg and touched his wallet.

He had taken some amphetamine earlier to keep himself going, but the grogginess didn't leave, and he yearned for something else.

All he could figure, they were wearing him down. Letting him stew. Letting him think about Marilyn. Letting him worry until he would meet on their terms, no questions asked. Waiting, he examined the diary. Chinese script, the paper moldy in places, ink-spotted and stained. It was dog-eared, and tucked into the middle was a piece of legal paper, Chinese symbols taken from the text, along with a handful of names, these written in English. Yin's notes, done with the assistance of his young friend. Some of the names Dante recognized, and some he didn't. They were the kind of names to be expected: a state senator, the attorney general, the head of a firm in Silicon Valley. Dante could figure out the specifics if he had enough time, but in a lot of ways, the specifics didn't matter. Yin had figured a link between the dayworld and the underground, between the shadowland where the company operated and the world of daily commerce. Chinese spies in the Silicon Valley, maybe. Heroin from Afghanistan. Saudi terrorists financed by American oil derivatives. Whatever it was, it linked prominent names to the underworld in which the company operated, endangering the organization itself. His guess, Yin had made contact with one of those names, seeking to exploit the knowledge to his own advantage. It might have worked. The company had not suspected Yin, but had come after Dante. They wanted their journal back. They could have it now, so far as Dante was concerned, but most likely his own innocence wouldn't matter.

Whatever stasis he had achieved, that was over now. He had been in the company. He had left. The initial betrayal alone had been reason enough to kill him, if not for the bargain he'd struck. Now that the bargain had been violated, it wouldn't matter who was responsible.

At last his phone rang.

He answered, expecting to hear that voice down there in the static, but the voice he heard belonged instead to his old friend Angelo, calling from downtown. His ex-partner's voice was gentle, as it sometimes could be, full of the neighborhood, of a brotherly concern he'd learned long ago to distrust.

"Where are you?"

"Out and about."

"We've been looking for you."

"That's sweet."

"I have bad news. Your boss, Jake Cicero. Maybe you heard?" Angelo did not wait for his answer. "That's three. Your cousin. The girl. Now Jake. All killed the same way."

"You talked to Louisa?"

"Yes, we talked to her."

"How is she?"

"Distraught. That's how she is. She said you called her place that evening, right around six. Looking for Jake."

"What are you getting at?"

"That matches time of death. I have a feeling." It was another one of their old lines, tongue in cheek, when the facts of a case, the coincidences, began to add up.

"So do I."

"Tell me where you are. Our feelings, we'll talk them over."

"I'm feeling a little shy."

"I would be, too, if I were you. You know, we can help you, and you can help us. But the longer you are out there, the longer you stay away. You know how it makes things look. The kind of feelings we get."

"I thought this was Chin's case."

"She's tied up."

"I can wait."

"We're working together. She asked me to call."

It was back to this. Technically, the various arms of enforcement all worked together, but Angelo had been under the gun lately, and though everybody talked about team effort, Angelo always had his own agenda.

"There are reasons," said Dante, "I'd rather talk to Chin."

"All right, I can see that. I'll have her call you." The sweetness in Angelo's voice reminded him of when they'd worked the streets together and used to sit after hours down in Serafina's, back when it had been a cop hangout, the two of them talking over old times, nudging elbows, staring down at the pictures of the old Italians embedded in the glass. Sweet as hell, one to the other, when they weren't rubbing each other the wrong way. "I don't want to see you go to hell," said Angelo.

Another old line, an old routine. Mocking the old priests, the nuns, and their playground admonitions.

"I might like it down there."

"I'm sure you would."

"You could visit."

"Like I said, I'll have her call you. You can set something up, just you and her."

In a little while, the phone rang back, just as Angelo

promised. Only it was not Chin herself, but an office underling, an anonymous voice, calling on behalf of her boss.

Chin would meet him tomorrow.

Dante went ahead with the arrangements, but he knew
better. If Chin wanted to arrange a meeting, she wouldn't go
through intermediaries. She would have made the arrangements herself. It wasn't Chin's underling making the arrangements, he suspected, but Angelo's.

Angelo had to know he would be suspicious. But his
friend was counting on his desperation, and his curiosity.
On his inability to leave anything alone.

The whore was back on the corner now, languid against
the wall. Dante looked past her, toward the freeway,
and felt the old yearning. It was a trap, that business with
Chin, he was all but sure, because Angelo wanted the collar
for himself. He wondered if Angelo had talked to the Feds,
and what kind of information had been passed along. Meanwhile, though, he had still heard nothing from the company, and he needed something to kill the pain in his leg.
He lit a cigarette and took in the smoke, tasting the ash and
heat in his throat.

He went across the street. He wasn't interested in the
girl, he told himself, but it would have been easy enough to
avoid her—if that's what he wanted. She wore a shift with a
cheap sheen, too thin for the weather, but when you got
close, the way she jittered, it didn't have so much to do with

the cold. Her face was mottled and her eyes had a different kind of yearning.

"Looking for a date?" she asked.

"No."

"Maybe you take me with you, then. Across the way, that's where you're going?"

He glanced past her toward the break in the fence that led to the shadows beneath the freeway.

"You remind me of someone."

"Oh, yeah," she said, cocking her hips. It was something all the johns said, he supposed, and her response, maybe, was always to move her hips just this way.

"A dancer. She worked at Gino's."

"I can dance, too. That's what you want."

Overhead, the traffic headed back the other way at this hour, northbound across the bridges, away from the asphalt canyons, the high towers, back toward all those houses nestled beside one another on the other side of the Bay.

"What do you want, then?"

"Nothing."

"That's sad."

"Not if it's true."

"I thought about working at Gino's." She glanced winsomely over at the freeway, as if it were impossible to be a junkie and work at a place like Gino's, so far across town.

"I need fifty bucks," she said.

He didn't need to ask why. A horn blared in the exit. Overhead the noise from the freeway, all those cars heading home, had become too much, and he wanted to find that empty space inside the noise. He felt sorry for the girl. Or she reminded him of the dead stripper. Of other women with whom he had walked in moments like this, in similar places. "No," he said, but either she did not hear, or something in his manner was not convincing. The prostitute hustled alongside him, squeezing through the place where the fence had been cut. Her dress seemed to shimmer a little more in the darkness under the freeway. Maybe it was the light shooting along the ramps, the glinting of the headlamps catching her as she moved, just ahead of him now, toward the hooded figure who stood alone, waiting. Then she backed off, letting him make the purchase. She knew the decorum. It was yet noisier here, not worth talking—and it was all pantomime now. Dante showed his money, and the hooded figure eased away, nodding imperceptibly toward one of the runners, a kid in a baseball cap twisted sideways, his long legs set in motion, off scampering to the stash. In another minute, Dante was on his knees, his nose in the powder, the woman kneeling beside him, her shoulder against his. His body went loose, suffuse with a sudden warmth, and he leaned against a nearby buttress, and after a while rolled over onto the ground. The woman lay a few feet away, reclining in the sparkling tinfoil. He closed his eyes. Back in New Orleans, in Armstrong Park, behind the gravestones. In a rickshaw, in Bangkok, head lolling as the cyclist pedaled over the Chao Phraya. In Spokane, under the railroad trestle.

He had been many places during his life with the company. Now, lying in the foil, he went there again.

⟨⟩

The woman accompanied him to his hotel room above the liquor store. He did not ask her to come, but he did not stop her either. He had made another purchase, and she followed. He took some comfort in her presence.

"No prostitutes," the clerk said.

"I'm his wife."

"No, you're not."

"We're just going to talk," said Dante.

"No visitors after ten. No whores. No double occupancy."

"I'm not a whore."

"No drugs."

Upstairs, the woman took off her panties but did not remove the dress. She positioned herself over him. The room was dark, the switch off, but light poured in anyway, past the flimsy curtains on their sagging rod. *Moonlight*, he thought, but that did not seem possible, given how the freeway trundled along the roofline, blocking the sky. Though the girl's features were masked, back there in the shadows, her arms, her shoulders, her neck, her skin, all had an alabaster glow. She arched her back, and he reached out to touch her breasts. She could be anyone. He saw in her eyes that little house in Marin, with the bedroom that opened onto the flagstone patio. He saw the square on the other side of the ocean. Meanwhile, the freeway thrummed in the walls. The girl moaned, an imperfect sound, touching herself on the belly as she did so. Then came down with her open mouth on his cock.

She lifted her head from between his legs. The moon was in her eyes.

"I'm so high," she said.

Later, she lay on the bed beside him. He expected she would leave any minute, but she was too high and fell instead into a dead sleep. The light poured through the window. The light was white, and everything else was black. The light was unadorned. The woman did not move, but lay silent with the light draped over her like a sheet.

Dante lay on the bed.

His leg no longer hurt.

He lay with one leg straddled over the bed and his arm hanging down and his head to the side. The light danced along the floor. There were blocks of darkness on the floor, rivers of light. A black city with avenues of white. Every thing was simple. There was nothing else, just the blackness and the light. Outside, a moth fluttered at the glass. The streets were naked, empty of desire.

"Marilyn," he said.

In the morning, his ache returned. It was the gray light coming through the window. The woman was gone. She had taken his dope—and his wallet, too.

But she had left the gun.

THIRTY-FIVE

The meeting place was along the Bay, past a line of corrugated huts out by Hunters Point. There had been a warehouse out here, but that had been torn down years ago, and all that remained was a ramshackle pier with the bench at the end where he was supposed to meet Chin. He did not walk out there but crouched in the brambles on a stone jetty, some half mile across the muddy inlet, a pile of rocks and concrete sprayed with graffiti. The brambles covered the jetty. Crackheads came here to get high, and faggots to suck each other off, but there was no one here at the moment and Dante lay alone in the brambles. The dope had worn off and the pain returned, but he still had amphetamines and also some Vicodin he'd gotten with some stray cash, tucked into his old pants, that the prostitute had not found. He focused on the fisherman who stood on the rotting pier across the way, a tall man in a hooded slicker, who reeled his line in, then cast once again into the water.

The man fished with his back toward Dante, off the opposite side of the pier.

For a long time, it was just the fisherman out there.

Then a car pulled up, stopped at the pier. The driver did not get out, not right away. Man or woman, Dante could not tell, just a shape behind the wheel. It was a colorless vehicle, plain and dull, of the type enforcement officials might use. It matched, too, the description of the vehicle Cicero had seen out the window.

Dante knew the history of the pier. The warehouse here had been owned by a German family, German Jews. During those first few months after the invasion of Pearl Harbor, the army had gone door to door, rousting out foreign nationals who owned property along the coast, and the warehouse that had stood here, it was one of those properties seized. With the help of Mayor Rossi, a young attorney back then—hand over his heart, saluting the flag—Dante's father and his uncle had made sure this place stayed closed. The city stopped dredging here, let the place fill with silt, and the war trade went through the Mancuso warehouse instead. His grandfather, nose like his nose, the Sicilian fisherman, got a piece of the shrimp trade, down at China camp.

We are all fish, the old man whispered. *We all get caught in the net.*

But it wasn't just that. During the war, there were certain needs. Medical supplies from fascist Chile, morphine by way of Singapore. Covert trade, arranged by government agents. Nobody cared about that anymore, just as no one would care later about whatever business was going on now.

A woman got out of the gray vehicle, across the inlet, and stepped onto the decaying pier: a dark-haired woman, with sunglasses, in a long coat to protect her from the wind. She might have been Chin, but he could not tell from this distance. She wore her collar turned up and had her back to him as she headed out toward the bench. The way she walked, it was not Chin's walk, but he could not be sure.

Perhaps the fisherman was just a fisherman.

The woman sat there patiently, well past the meeting time, and he was tempted to walk out. Part of him wanted to trust Angelo. It would be easier that way. Because if the woman was Chin, he could hand her the journal, he could seek asylum . . . and for a minute he allowed himself to believe that such a thing was possible, that there was a straight and narrow, and all he had to do was follow it. That his friend would not sell him out. That Chin could help him. The woman leaned back, arms spread across the bench, but it was not Chin, he knew now for certain, because the fisherman came and sat down beside her.

He watched the fisherman load his gear in the trunk and he watched the woman, too, and he knew who they were.

He lay in the brambles.

The phone rang.

The line was full of static and white noise. With that same hollow clicking, persistent but growing faint. When the insect spoke, the voice was tinny and cruel, as always, but that cruelness seemed tinged with melancholy.

"You were a good agent once."

"Where is she?"

"Untouched."

"How do I know that?"

"You could be a good agent again, given the opportunity."

"Let her go."

"You have it wrong. At this point, we are only monitoring. We know where she is, let's put it that way. But I think it would be better if we work together."

"You want the journal."

"The only reason to kill her would be to punish you. To set an example."

There was a hint of weariness there. As if the insect were disappointed that Dante had not done it the easy way. That he had not simply handed over the journal and allowed himself to be strangled at the end of the pier. But the insect was practical. He hid his disappointment. "It is better to put this in the past," he said. "We have need of you. It is better we make a deal."

THIRTY-SIX

The New Asia was down off Vallejo, around the corner from the Serafina. An elegant place, Chinese, but without the smells of Chinatown. No old yellow men in gray trousers. No raw-handed women, stinking of skewered chicken. The New Asia did not cater to that group, and anyway they wouldn't come. The prices were too expensive and the crowd too young, just off work, up from the finance houses on Kearney. The place had an international look, no pictures of the neighborhood along the wall, no memorabilia, just the sleek black surfaces polished until they reflected the visitor's own face back.

Dante's instructions had been simple: Go sit at the bar. Two drinks, one for yourself, whatever you like, and a vodka tonic, Grey Goose over ice. In a while, someone will come and sit next to you, in front of that drink. You will hand them the diary. Then you will walk away, back out the way you came. Your girl will be left alone. All you have to do, after that, is everything we ask.

He'd agreed, in essence, to disappear into oblivion. To do their every bidding. To take his old job back.

We have need of you. You were a good agent once.

Dante did not trust the insect. Neither did he have a lot of choices. He turned on his stool, surveying the crowd. From the back, alone at the table, a man regarded him: a tall, wide-shouldered man in a sport jacket, with bland good looks. He nodded, a comradely nod, that could have meant anything at all. He had the type of looks, change his clothes, he could be anyone. A tourist in a Windbreaker, walking with his wife to the top of Telegraph Hill. Some guy from the financial district, going over his notes at the end of the day. A fisherman at the end of a pier.

The woman entered the bar. She was dark-haired like the woman on the bench, out at the pier, only her hair hung loose and the clothes were not the same. She was no longer masquerading, at least not in the same way. Put her in a polo shirt, a camera around her neck, curl the hair, she and the man behind him, they could ride a cable car all day. Wander up to Coit Tower. Walk in Cicero's office, a divorcée and her lover. Strangle his cousin on Telegraph Hill.

Dante had met her before, she and the man behind him, that day out in Marin, Marilyn's clients, the couple she'd been showing around.

"Is that mine?"

"You tell me."

She leaned over, tasted it. "Grey Goose."

"Yes."

"You look a little out of place here, a man like you."

"You mean that as a compliment?"

"Take it how you will."

It was the kind of game they played, the company, banter like this. He didn't have the stomach for it right now, but he played anyway. Meanwhile, the clientele in the bar, they bantered, too. From the looks of them, they owned the world, these people. A young crowd, mixed race, bound by nothing. They hailed from everywhere and nowhere. The woman next to him, she fit right in. She had eyes that might have been Asian, but then again it could have been the way her eyebrows were done. Her lips had a touch of the negroid. Her skin was dark, but not too dark. Native American, maybe, or Filipina, Hawaiian. Then, too, maybe just a white girl with exotic earrings. Skin tinted in a tanning salon, the way they were doing these days.

The man in the back, he had the same looks, more or less. Dante preferred Nelson Yin. Or Chin. Even Angelo. These new ones, you could drive a knife into them, split them up the middle, watch the lips curl up and the blood pour—and even then, you still wouldn't know who they were.

"That's your associate, at the table behind me."

"Does it matter?"

"You did a good job, you two. All this time circling, so close, watching, but I didn't see."

"The journal . . ."

"But you had help, didn't you?"

The woman shrugged.

"Angelo."

"He's just a cop," she said. "He whispers to his friends in the Feds. Whispers get passed along—but you know all that. I don't mean to be impatient, but you understand why I'm here."

"The journal, yes. How do you know I haven't made copies?"

"The information, once we have that, once we know what is being alleged, the people who need protecting, we find avenues."

"So it doesn't matter."

"You know, deep down, the journal was only part of it."

She smiled, dismissive, but he'd gotten her gist. The company did not like its people playing both sides. On the phone, the insect had been almost polite, apologetic. Willing to make a deal. Let bygones be bygones. *We have need of you.* He was a lucky man. She leaned over then and whispered to him. As she whispered, he felt the hot breath in his ear and a cringe at the back of his neck.

"Do you love her?"

He did not like the question, nor did he like the light in her eyes.

She was enjoying herself, lingering over her drink. She bent closer and ran her long finger down his nose. "This is how I knew you were the man," she said, "by your nose."

"Marilyn," Dante said. "I want to know she's all right."

She reached into her purse and showed a series of pictures that had been e-mailed to her cell, a grainy sequence of shots. A woman walking in a foreign square. A cobbled alley.

A basilica. From a distance, the woman looked like Marilyn, but up close, in profile, he had his doubts. Then another shot, the woman standing on a motel balcony, in a white slip, overlooking the beach. A shadow filled the door behind her, a man, perhaps David Lake, but no, Lake would do better. In the final picture, the motel had a touch of shabbiness about it, and there was a vendor cart selling *helados*, in the lower corner, a tired-looking woman pushing it across the highway. *Ensenada,* he realized. They had followed the wrong woman. He tried to keep the realization out of his face.

"How did you find her?" he asked.

"The airport," she said, and he remembered then the gray car snaking down the access road when he'd driven out to SFO with Marilyn's look-alike beside him.

The woman finished her drink. The bartender came by, and the woman raised her eyebrows, as if she were ready to have another, as if she would sit all night, but by the end of it, nothing would be any different, because if he did not cooperate . . .

The woman smiled. It was not a smile he liked. "Do you want to give it to me?"

The insect's deal, it was no deal at all, not really. *We need you, an assignment,* and for that they would let Marilyn be. In the end, nevertheless, there was no guarantee. Sooner or later, they would figure out the woman in Ensenada was not Marilyn. The woman's eyes had that bright shine—like the first time he'd met her, out in Marin. Too bright. He turned sideways on his stool.

"It's a tough fix, isn't it?"

"I could just walk out."

"You could. But we'd find you."

"There's other options," he said, and he put his hand in his pocket. His other option was to kill them both, this woman in front of him, that man at the table, and to be on the next plane out. To move before they moved. The woman brushed the hair from her eyes. He could put his gun in the brunette's stomach and shoot her friend, too, before he'd risen to his toes. But he did not know where the real Marilyn was.

"You'll never make it to the airport."

"I might."

"If I don't walk out of here with that journal," said the woman, "if our man doesn't hear from us . . . you'll never see her again."

It was a hollow threat. They had the wrong woman, but they didn't know that.

"They're waiting for my call."

"Of course," he said.

Better to let them win. Or think they had. The journal was nothing to him. He gave it to the woman. She took the journal as if it were nothing and slid it in the side pocket of her jacket. "I imagine the police are looking for you."

"I imagine."

"Before you leave the city, there's a package for you. Back at your hotel."

"My assignment?"

She smiled once more, lingering for a final moment over

her drink, regarding him in a way that suggested it was not over, not quite, not really, and he imagined her giving the same look to Cicero, and to his cousin. Then she swallowed the rest of her Grey Goose and headed for the street.

THIRTY-SEVEN

Outside, the world had its same color, and it was tempting to think now everything might go on as before. An Asian couple came down the walk toward him, slicked up to the nines, sheer and well made. Jazz fell from a window overhead, and an aging hipster staggered down the way. Along Stockton, the buildings were red with twilight. The evening glistened.

Dante had walked along the streets so often, it was easy to fool himself into thinking he would walk them forever. That they were his in some irrevocable way.

His high had worn down to the point of desire, and his leg hurt. He lit a cigarette, then pushed deeper into Chinatown, onto the thronged walkways, the strangers parting half-heartedly, bumping shoulders, pushing this way and that, the air thick with the smell of ginger and pig fat and rotting poultry.

After the woman left the bar, Dante had sat for a long moment in the New Asia, with the drink in front of him. The man at the back table had vanished as well. Seemingly, everything was settled. The company had their journal. Marilyn was safe, off with David Lake. As for him, his next assignment lay waiting ahead.

Still, he was filled with unease.

In Portsmouth Square, the pigeons squabbled beneath the benches, and magnolia leaves littered the walk. Most of the day people had cleared out, but a couple of old Chinamen persisted, coats buttoned to the collar, hovering about the stone chess table. Farther on, a cruiser parked across from the nameless hotel, and he saw what looked like an unmarked car at the mouth of the alley, by the iron gate.

It didn't necessarily mean anything. There were always cops around.

A package for you, back at the hotel.

The woman had flirted, smiled insidiously, letting him know, if not now, then eventually, the trap would spring. That sooner or later, his utility would wear thin.

A bullet in the back of the head. A knife in the stomach. A fall from a parking structure.

Meanwhile, Dominick Greene was still lying in the basement back at Serafina's, among the canned tomatoes, in the blocked tunnel. Once upon a time, those tunnels had led everywhere. There were a million stories, and in one of those stories, a fugitive had swapped his identity with that of a corpse, and disappeared through those tunnels.

Those tunnels, the old-timers said, went all the way to Italy.

Now, up ahead, he could see the million Buddhas in the lobby window, and back in the dim light the Russian behind the desk. Inside, the Russian sat with his package of Kools on the counter, posed in what looked to have been the identical position as before, behind the hotel desk, surrounded by the many Buddhas. The Buddha of tranquillity. The Buddha of sexual foreplay. Of the lecherous grin. Of the insatiable appetite.

The place was empty of customers, as it was always empty.

"There is something here for you."

The Russian turned to the bank of slotted cubbyholes behind the long desk, a structure left from the days when lodgers dropped their room keys with the clerk and visitors left handwritten messages, tucked and folded, stashed into those little boxes. The slots were all empty now, full of dust, but the Russian pulled a package from the shelf below: a smallish box, wrapped in brown paper.

"Who dropped it off?"

"I was out."

"That's unusual."

"I have to eat lunch sometime," he said. "I have to take a crap."

The lobby man looked like someone accustomed to lying, so even if he was telling the truth, you would not know. It was clear the man had no intention of speaking on the matter further. Dante knew how it went: You got the job, you figured out how things worked—and then you shut up. You sat quietly. You took a little money on the side, and you aligned yourself with the forces that were going to win regardless.

What fool would do otherwise?

Dante took the package upstairs. He paused at the top of the hall and looked out at the street. The unmarked car was still there at the mouth of the alley, and the squad car sat as before. He imagined the couple up at the Stanford Hotel, at the top of Nob Hill, pausing at the window to look at the city below them. Then down the elevator, into the taxi, in their anonymous Windbreakers, cameras around their necks, off to the airport, the next city, the next open house.

Dante went down the hall into the room. It still smelled of the old woman, but of himself now, too. He put the package on the bed and checked his gun and peered into the alley. There was no moon. The light the evening before, that naked glow pouring in through the hotel window, had issued from an arc lamp beneath the freeway.

Dante stripped away the brown wrapping and the white string to reveal the box beneath, a cardboard mailer, the size of a shirt box, itself as of yet unopened. It had been sent international express from Mexico, judging from the markings on the outside, though the mailing bill had been stripped away.

The inside package was soft with padding, packed with tissue, spotted in places, scabby and damp. Inside the wrapping: a white nightgown, gauze thin. Slashed and stained with blood.

A noise came from somewhere. A low keening; a rolling wail; laughter almost, but not laughter, not at all; a sound not quite human. Or too human. Dante himself could not tell where it came from. From down below somewhere. From the night streets out there, Angelo and his squad car friends. Chin. Up out of the black dirt, from the hollow in his chest. He understood now. The woman in the cell phone picture. The lace gown. The shadow in the background.

They had killed Marilyn. Or the woman they thought was Marilyn. Down in Ensenada.

There was nothing inside him. The noise had emptied out of him, and in the middle of that emptiness, again, the ringing of his cell.

"We know you are up there," said Angelo. "You should come down. It could be messy otherwise."

Dante stood in the hall, at the window overlooking the street. Angelo was at the squad car, and his thick-necked partner, Sergeant Jones, lounged against the unmarked sedan. There were other shadows in the square as well, moving, and heading from the corner he saw Chin, in a hurry, crossing against the traffic. Angelo did not seem pleased to see her, and the way she confronted him, Dante saw her urgency, her fury. She was late to the party, not of her own accord, Dante guessed, but because she had not been informed, at least not by Angelo. Dante saw how it was. Angelo had been tipped to his presence here, and his friends at the company, they'd never intended to let him off so easy.

THIRTY-EIGHT

Dante dropped down into the alley. The drop had been hard enough two days back, when he'd first explored the alley, before he'd taken the scissors in the leg. When he landed, the pain shot back up into his thigh, up through the groin. He lingered an instant in his crouch, like a wounded cat, staring warily down into the far recess, where the alley narrowed. There were only two ways to go: toward the iron gate, where the thick-necked sergeant was waiting, or back into the alley.

He went toward the street first. On this side of the gate, there stood a pair of Dumpsters fed by a restaurant whose employees had access from the other side, but the access was one-way. He peered through the iron gate at Sergeant Jones sitting sentry in the unmarked car.

Dante headed back into the alley.

There was a parapet up along the ledge, and behind that parapet a little stone recess, big enough for a man to hide in.

Something shifted in the blackness up there, along the parapet, but he could not be sure. He went deeper into the alley, more slowly now, softly, stilling his breath.

The look in the woman's eyes, there at the bar . . .

He hesitated at the place where the corridor narrowed then bent back on itself, turning, then turning again, the passageway growing blacker with each turn. The alley ended in a small clearing, if you wanted to call it that, an asphalt patch between buildings where the old Chinaman, the gatekeeper, kept his bedroll.

He stopped at the final corner.

A dim light flickered against the brick ahead, and there was a sound, like a broken record, a humming, a man about to sing but stuck on the opening syllable. Dante edged along the alley wall, and as he did so, his view widened. He did not see the old Chinaman at first, and when he did see him, it was not so much the man himself as the shape of the man, tucked back in the recess of a farther alcove, illuminated dimly, momentarily, by a can of Sterno at the head of the arch. The old man was meditating, and the moans came from him, some old chant, by no means sonorous. Dante stepped out into the open area. It was no more really than a shaft between buildings. At this angle the old man was no longer visible. The Sterno threw vague shadows against the brick along the opposite wall, and he had an impression of someone moving in those shadows. There was a narrow walkway on the other side of the Chinaman, but it went nowhere, a shoulder-width passage, brick on both sides, that sloped down to a metal drain. He heard a shuffling back there, rats, and then another noise, as of someone dropping into the larger alley—from that parapet, perhaps—back in the direction from which he had just come.

Dante had been here in daylight. The fire escape dropped from above, down the shaft, ending prematurely, a flight above. At the point where the fire stairs broke off, an iron slat remained embedded horizontally into the brick. He had to strain to reach this, then plant his feet against the wall, arching his spine, looking for purchase, all the while reaching with the free hand for the bottom of the ladder. He heard a noise behind him. Pain shot up his leg. He pushed through it, grasping upward. In the same instant, he heard a click behind him, the cock of the chamber, a soft female grunt. The old man was still meditating. Dante heard another set of footsteps behind him, a third presence, emerging from the corridor down which he himself had just come. He realized it now, who they were. He reached for his holster as he hung one-handed from the ladder, twisting. Then his leg gave out and he fell. He landed raggedly, falling to one knee, with the other leg sprawled behind and two hands on the ground.

"Up," the woman said. "Arms away."

The woman stood with the gun pointed at his chest. The man, her good-looking friend, he circled behind. The same couple, of course. Angelo was but an instrument, a prod. Still waiting out front, knowing, as these two knew, that Dante would not willingly emerge—but instead take this last avenue. If he hadn't, if he had gone out to Angelo, no doubt his old friend would have surrendered him all the same.

Angelo had whispered to his friends in Federal, and the whispers had traveled, the way whispers do. Dante could hear the insect hissing down there in the center of hell: *Make him unwrap that package . . . before he dies. . . . Bury his face in the bloody dress.* He had outwitted them three years ago, but in the end, no one betrayed the company. Do so, and they took your life away from you, piece by piece, and then when it was all gone, they came for you. They didn't know, not yet, they'd gotten the wrong woman, down in Ensenada. Meanwhile, the old Chinaman went on meditating. Angelo leaned against his squad car out front, and Chin . . .

The woman gave him the same smile he'd seen in the bar. They could have gotten him more simply, these two. They could have put a gun to his head and killed him in the street. But, no. They enjoyed their work, and the message it sent. The man, he loved the feeling of the dowel in his hands, loved that moment just ahead, when he would pull the wire tight, and this woman, with the gun in her hand, she loved to watch.

Overhead, a light flicked on, off. A window opened. He could rush the woman, or pull his gun. She would have to shoot him in the stomach, kill him that way, but it was too late. What happened next, happened in an instant. Dante heard the rustle of fabric behind him, the man in motion. It was the moment toward which everything had been moving, he understood that now, the moment he would not escape. The woman sighed. He heard a snap of wire and the whistle of the air. It was too late even to reach for his gun. As the wire whistled down, he did the only thing that remained. He ducked. He let his body collapse toward his knees—and at the same moment, he raised his hand.

The rope caught him anyway.

It caught his hand at the palm, and his fingers were trapped there, under the wire, up against his neck. He felt his head twist back, wire in the throat, feet lifting from the ground. The man turned, bending, and the rope cinched, biting deeper. His feet left the ground altogether now. His neck twisted—there was a noise . . . a sudden cracking . . . a flash of white. . . .

THIRTY-NINE

In the moment of death, there are a million eternities—or so the nuns had told him—the seconds divided into milliseconds, infinite divisions, in which the brain denies its own demise. As in the schoolboy story—one he had read as a child—the soldier on the gallows sees the calvary on the near hill—the marksman's shot slices the hanging rope—and the self falls through the trick door into the continuing illusion of its own existence. Something like this, maybe, had happened in this moment, Dante would think later, stumbling. *I am not dead.* The voice coming from above sounded real enough.

"Halt!"

It happened so quickly, he could not be sure. The warning shot, and then the voice, a dark form peering down from the lighted window farther up the shaft. Dante recognized the voice. Chin. She had left off arguing with Angelo and circled around on her own, perhaps, coming through the adjoining building. Dante saw himself as if from the window above, flailing absurdly, panicky, gasping, grabbing with both hands at the rope as the man bent deeper, and the wire tightened, cutting into his own throat.

I am not dead.

The voice from above . . . or the mind deceiving itself . . . His heart beat impossibly fast. . . . His mind raced. . . . Then came the exchange of fire, the blackness streaked with light, the gunshots echoing in the small alley as if inside his skull. Inside that alley, that blackness, the woman whirled, firing into the light, and the light fired back. He felt the man stagger beneath him, and his own body go loose, slack, prickling all over. A pain flared in his shoulder. Then suddenly he slid free, twisting in midair, hitting the ground like a sack dumped in the alley. He lay motionless in the dark, with a great heaviness on his chest, as if all the air had been pushed out. Somehow, in the fall, Dante had ended up on the bottom with the man on top. The man had been shot in the skull. It was quiet, only the Sterno for light, and Dante glimpsed the woman leaning against the brick with her long fingers over a wound in her stomach. The woman slid down the brick, holding her stomach. The gun had fallen from her hand, but she did not take her eyes off Dante. Her face was going white, her exotic looks draining away. Her lip curled and hung low, and her chin lengthened as the death shudder ran through her, but she kept those eyes fixed on Dante, as if it were not her that was dying, but him, his body clenching, and as he let loose, at last, the light in her eyes receded until it vanished altogther, dwindling in the darkness of the shaft. He gathered all his strength and pushed the dead man off his chest.

A bove him, he heard voices, bystanders, the unruly chatter of the apartment dwellers as they peered down into the alley, curious, frightened—switching on lights, switching them off, yelling contradictory instructions—in the center of that confusion was the window from which the voice had issued, and the gunfire as well. He expected Chin to call down, but he heard instead the static of the citizen band, a cop radio, and a faint voice, a woman, radioing for help.

"Officer down. Need assistance here. I'm bleeding."

The voice belonged to Chin. She had not been invited, no, but she'd looped around the back, spoiling the party. She had killed the man and the woman, and in the process taken fire herself. Dante had been hit in the shoulder during the firefight.

Dante took the journal from the dead woman's pocket. At the other end of the alley, on the near side of the iron gate, he encountered Angelo, hovering as if in a dream, a little boy, an Italian kid in the alley in a strange part of town where he'd come despite himself, unable to stay away.

Dante held the gun in his good hand.

"No," Angelo said.

Behind him, Dante heard the sound of the Chinaman meditating in the alley, the same mantra, over and over. It had been there in the background, all the while, persistent, unceasing. Looking up, through the stairwell window, he caught a glimpse of Sergeant Jones pounding the stairs upward into the hotel. Angelo backed away. He raised his hands. Dante could smell him, the sweat in his nappy hair, a smell like his boyhood streets.

"No," Angelo said.

"Of course not," Dante said. "I would never do such a thing."

"I knew you wouldn't."

The old routine, it never ended.

He shot Angelo in the stomach.

Then he took out the key the Russian had given him a few days before and unlocked the iron gate.

FORTY

Dante weaved up through the street, past the Wu Temple. He limped as before, only worse, dragging his foot behind him—and he was also bleeding from the shoulder. He wore a kimono, taken from a street rack on Grant Street, but the blood seeped through, and his hair and face were flecked, too, with blood from the dead man. People looked in his direction but did not seem to see him, even as the crowd thickened, down along the slope toward Vallejo. There was a logical explanation for this, he told himself. People in Chinatown, their eyes avoided trouble. The crowd always thickened through here, but it was tighter now. Still he slid through—as if he were a ghost passing through. A rally clotted the street. With the surge from Gennae Rossi, and the incumbent's troubles, the race had tightened, and Lee's people were beating the drum. A white Ford, battered to hell, draped in bunting, a microphone over the hood, the sound of Chinese wailing up through the static. A giant papier-mâché worm, wiggling down the street. A dancing monkey. A woman holding a sign.

At Serafina's, Dante leaned against the darkened window. Stella had left everything as it was. The tables, the checkered cloths. The candles and the wineglasses and the painting of Mt. Vesuvius on the wall. Stella hadn't bothered to finish cleaning. There was a dirty plate over where Old Lady Besozi had been sitting, and a half-empty wine bottle on the bar. On that counter, underneath the bar top, all those photos, laminated behind the glass, old-timers and their Cadillacs, fat cigars, a thousand Polaroids, two thousand, any wop who'd ever walked through North Beach, his own mom and his dad and his grandfather with his pelican nose. Himself, Marilyn. Old Man Prospero and Gino and some dancing girl with her chest pushed out. Dante pressed his nose against the window, peered in, woozy, and in his heightened state, he imagined they were all in there at once, eating, drinking, rubbing shoulders. It was a celebration, like the old days, of the type that used to go on, and in the midst of that, Marilyn in her white dress, and himself, too, and everyone raising their glasses.

A vision of what might have been, maybe, his brain dizzy from loss of blood, lack of oxygen.

As he leaned there, staring into the glass, he almost believed it was possible. They had killed the wrong woman after all, down in Ensenada. All he had to do was pass through that glass. All he had to do was exchange his body for Dominick Greene's. Swap identities with the corpse in the tunnel.

Then he would find Marilyn. . . . But, no . . . there was no going back . . . even if it was not too late, and he could pry her away from David Lake . . .

They would follow.

There was only one way to keep her safe.

In the reflection, he saw the gash in his neck, and he poked his finger inside, feeling the cut. *I am not dead,* he told himself, though in truth, he did not have any other explanation for the way he felt just now. As if he were passing through that glass. As if he were down in that maze, pulling Greene by his arms, yanking him through the underground sewers, through the winemaker's tunnels, up toward his father's garage. The others would be coming soon, he knew that: the Federal agents and the bullyboys, the local cops and the Wus—and the only question was which of them would come first, and how many. They would not come gently, he knew that, too, and when they were done with him, there would be nothing left. They would seize it all, the family property: the house on Fresno, and his cousin's place and the business down at the wharf. They would let all the property sit empty for a while, letting the taxes run up, compounding penalties, and when there was no equity there, not a nickel for anyone to claim but the government, they'd sell it at auction to the highest bidder, with his family's junk still inside.

Dante stood in his father's house, in the basement. He had made it home. He did not have much time now.

After he was gone, all this stuff—these boxes of paper and bags of crockery and the tapestries and the unwanted furniture and his father's old clothes—would end up in the scavenger truck. The real estate agents wouldn't want it around. The new owners, someday, would drink coffee here and eat risotto and panini in commemoration of the people whom they imagined to have lived here, but the fact of the matter was, before any of that could happen, all that old stuff, with its musty smell, had to be gone first, removed from the house.

Dante reached inside the box containing the wedding ring his father had worn, given to him by his mother those many years ago. The old Italians—Pesci, Marinetti, Gino and Stella, Julia Besozi and all the rest—they all looked on in approval. *Into the tunnel.* Greene's corpse gave him the rictus smile.

Dante slid the ring on his finger.

He picked up the can of gasoline. It was a big can, and there was more gas in the big container under the bench. He dumped the gas on the boxes, on the clothes. He soaked it all good. *That's right, burn it all.* There was a furnace in the corner, with an electronic ignition, controlled by a thermostat upstairs. When you adjusted the thermostat, there was a lag of a couple minutes. Then the burner would ignite.

He took the other can and splashed gasoline all over the front room. All over the sofa and the RCA. His father's chair. Over the drapes and the counters.

He checked the pilot to the stove. Turned on the thermostat.

He climbed into the attic, a lurching, clumsy figure, hunched under the rafters, pouring the last of the gasoline. His mother's things now, the picture albums, endless photographs. Birth certificates and baptismal records, a wedding menu from the Fior d'Italia, a dance card issued by the Knights of Columbus, old 45s, Holy Communion cards and a ribbon he himself had won throwing javelin at an event sponsored by the Saints Peter and Paul Church.

He found at the last minute a list of passage, names of families who'd made the voyage, their names, the villages, compiled by the defunct newspaper, *L'Italia,* in the days before World War II. He touched the gash in his throat . . . too deep for him to be alive . . . in the moment of death, you wander the streets of your childhood . . . you suffer what you have lost. . . . *I am not dead.* . . . There was one way to keep them from following Marilyn. If he himself were forever beyond their reach, there would be no reason. They could not punish him by going after her.

Downstairs, the heater engaged.

He'd heard it engage, just like that, thousands of times.

Where had it started?

In the hold of those ships . . . lonely men, holding shovels . . .

There was a lull.

Marilyn.

A slight whooshing, as of a breeze through an open window. A bell rang somewhere. Then came the explosion, the sound of which carried out to the Bay, or so they said later. All of North Beach in flames, the whole city. Himself at the center, in the incendiary light.

The tunnel opened ahead.

FORTY-ONE

Several days later, when Leanora Chin got out of the hospital, the block still smoldered. The fire crew had struggled with the hydrant on Fresno, but in the end had to run the hoses in six different directions, over the hill and back around, in an effort to tap into the broken water main. Meantime the adjacent building went up, and the flames leaped to the wood-frame apartments on the corner.

The fire had spread across Grant and up Telegraph as well. Under control now, supposedly, though early morning, at dusk, the infrared cameras—in the news copters overhead—showed pockets that still burned.

The scene had a feeling of unreality. Chin had been wheeled out after the shoot-out, red lights spinning, paramedics calling ahead for blood. She'd been shot, her elbow shattered, and her body sliced by the falling glass. She had taken shards in the neck, and in the chest, and the blood ran down her white blouse and soaked her skirt. She'd had the feeling then as if nothing were real, as if she herself were being imagined—*I do not exist*—and remembered herself as a little girl, inside one of the temples in Chinatown, a vast temple, humming with emptiness, in the middle of that emptiness, an old monk whispering, but later, she wondered if the memory were true.

We are figures in a dream. The dreamer, too. You have no control.

She stood on Fresno Street now, with her arms in a sling. She was dressed in blue.

She wasn't healed, the wounds seeped beneath their pads, but she had wanted to be here when they pulled the body. It took a while. The house had fallen in on itself, and the forensic team had to dig through the charred rafters.

Last night, still in the hospital, she'd gotten a visit from the Feds, filling in the gaps, but the information they'd given her, the report to be filed, she knew certain aspects weren't true.

No matter, the news was full of it: examining the link between the man inside the house and the shoot-out in the alley, and the fire consuming the neighborhood.

TRAGEDY ROCKS ITALIAN NORTH BEACH, the paper said.

The story of the private detective gone mad. His rage triggered by some family ugliness, perhaps, or the fact that his fiancée had gone off with another man. Killing his cousin, his business partner. Invading the Wu Benevolent Association. Then, cornered by the police, there'd been a shoot-out in Chinatown. According to the news reports, two tourists had been caught in the cross fire, and a policeman slain as well.

A bizarre killing streak that had spiraled out of control, then ending when the man burned himself alive in the family home.

The truth of the matter was more illusory. Chin knew the story didn't check. The dead couple in the alley, they were not tourists—of this, she was positive—but she'd been given instructions: Say nothing. Meanwhile, the news was all over the television. A time line of the killings, maps with special insets, interviews with old-timers, the parish priest, a psychologist who specialized in understanding such rampages. And tales, too, of the fire burning while voters went to the polls.

An election-day circus. The city gone out of control.

The stories had not helped Gennae Rossi, the neighborhood girl, but the votes that might have gone to her, they did not go to Lee either.

On the front page, in the midst of it all, the incumbent stood, sleeves rolled, helping at the fire line. Everything changed, but nothing at all. He, too, Chin knew, was financed by the Wus. They spread their money to every candidate, taking no chances.

The forensics team found the bones. The fire had burned the body beyond recognition, but the dentals were intact. The body was the right size, and there was a ring, on the wedding finger, fused to the bone.

Angelo had been in touch with the Feds before the shoot-out; she knew that now. Angelo had learned that Dante was going to be there, in that old hotel, and positioned himself for the arrest. Angelo had arranged it on his own, telling her nothing. She'd found out at the last minute that Angelo was there, staking out the scene, planning the arrest. Something was wrong about it, she'd thought: how he'd waited, how there was no one stationed at the alley around back. So she'd gone herself, moving through the dream-dark street, under the yellow neon, up the steps of the adjoining hotel. Peering down into the darkened shaft. Nothing at first, just the Sterno flashing, odd shadows against the brick. A voice, her own, calling down into that darkness. Then came the exchange of fire, the exploding glass.

The Feds had sent their own forensics people, and they were moving in now, taking over the remains. Chin shouldered her way in.

"We'll do the analysis," the man said.

"It's my case."

"No," the man said. "He's ours."

The breeze stirred. Barricades had been placed at the street, but there weren't enough personnel, and the press tumbled through and gawkers as well, and up the street an anonymous old man, rummaging the embers, had started to weep. Some chimes turned in the wind, and an aria echoed from a radio, somewhere, full of static, and there was a noise, too, she thought, like water slapping at the side of a boat. It was dusk, and the sounds of barkers carried up from Broadway. Chin took a last look at the figure spread on the blue cloth, and was tempted to remove the ring from the man's finger. She clenched her empty hand, then headed into Chinatown. The streets were filled with ash.

ML

3/10